BURGLARS
CAN'T BE
CHOOSERS

Other books by Lawrence Block

THE BERNIE RHODENBARR SERIES

The Burglar in the Closet
The Burglar Who Liked to Quote Kipling
The Burglar Who Studied Spinoza
The Burglar Who Painted Like Mondrian
The Burglar Who Traded Ted Williams
The Burglar Who Thought He Was Bogart
The Burglar in the Library
The Burglar in the Rye
The Burglar on the Prowl
The Burglar Who Counted the Spoons
The Burglar in Short Order

THE MATTHEW SCUDDER SERIES

The Sins of the Fathers
In the Midst of Death
Time to Murder and Create
A Stab in the Dark
Eight Million Ways to Die
When the Sacred Ginmill Closes
Out on the Cutting Edge
A Ticket to the Boneyard
A Dance at the Slaughterhouse
A Walk Among the Tombstones
The Devil Knows You're Dead
A Long Line of Dead Men
Even the Wicked
Everybody Dies
Hope to Die
All the Flowers Are Dying
A Drop of the Hard Stuff
A Time to Scatter Stones

BURGLARS CAN'T BE CHOOSERS

LAWRENCE BLOCK

Reader's
Digest

New York / Montreal

THE BEST MYSTERIES OF ALL TIME

BURGLARS CAN'T BE CHOOSERS

For Steve and Nancy Schwerner

Burglars Can't Be Choosers

Chapter One

A HANDFUL of minutes after nine I hoisted my Bloomingdale's shopping bag and moved out of a doorway and into step with a tall blond fellow with a faintly equine cast to his face. He was carrying an attaché case that looked too thin to be of much use. Like a high-fashion model, you might say. His topcoat was one of those new plaid ones and his hair, a little longer than my own, had been cut a strand at a time.

"We meet again," I said, which was an out-and-out lie. "Turned out to be a pretty fair day after all."

He smiled, perfectly willing to believe that we were neighbors who exchanged a friendly word now and then. "Little brisk this evening," he said.

I agreed that it was brisk. There wasn't much he might have said that I wouldn't have gladly agreed with. He looked respectable and he was walking east on Sixty-seventh Street and that was all I required of him. I didn't want to befriend him or play handball with him or learn the name of his barber or coax him into swapping shortbread recipes. I just wanted him to help me get past a doorman.

The doorman in question was planted in front of a seven-story brick building halfway down the block, and he'd been very nearly as stationary as the building itself during the past half-hour. I'd given him that much time to desert his post and he hadn't taken advantage of it, so now I was going to have to walk right past him. That's easier than it sounds, and it's certainly easier than the various alternatives I'd considered earlier—circling the block and going through another building to get into the airshaft behind the building I wanted, doing a human fly act onto the fire escape, torching my way through steel grilles on basement or first-floor windows. All of those things are possible, I suppose, but so what? The proper method is Euclidean in its simplicity: the shortest route into a building is through its front door.

I'd hoped that my tall blond companion might be a resident of the building himself. We could have continued our conversation, such as it was, right through the lobby and onto the elevator. But this was not to be. When it was clear that he was not going to turn from his eastward course I said, "Well, here's where I get off. Hope that business in Connecticut works out for you."

This ought to have puzzled him, as we hadn't talked about any business in Connecticut or elsewhere, but perhaps he assumed I'd mistaken him for someone else. It hardly mattered. He kept on walking toward Mecca while I turned to my right (toward Brazil), gave the doorman a quick unfocused nod and smile, warbled a pleasant "Good evening" at a gray-haired woman with more than the traditional number of chins, chuckled unconvincingly when her Yorkie made snapping sounds at my heels, and strode purposefully onto the self-service elevator.

I rode to the fourth floor, poked around until I found the stairway, and walked down a flight. I almost always do this and sometimes wonder why. I think someone must have done it in a movie once and I was evidently impressed, but it's really a waste of time, especially when the elevator in question is self-service. The one thing it does is fix in your mind where the stairs are, should you later need them in a hurry, but you ought to be able to locate stairs without scampering up or down them.

On the third floor, I found my way to Apartment 311 at the front of the building. I stood for a moment, letting my ears do the walking, and then I gave the bell a thorough ring and waited thirty thoughtful seconds before ringing it again.

And that, let me assure you, is not a waste of time. Public institutions throughout the fifty states provide food and clothing and shelter for lads who don't ring the bell first. And it's not enough just poking the silly thing. A couple of years back I rang the bell diligently enough at the Park Avenue co-op of a charming couple named Sandoval, poked the little button until my finger throbbed, and wound up going directly to jail without passing Go. The bell was out of order, the Sandovals were home scoffing toasted English muffins in the breakfast nook, and Bernard G. Rhodenbarr soon found himself in a little room with bars on the windows.

This bell was in order. When my second ring brought no more response than my first, I reached a hand beneath my topcoat—last year's model, not plaid but olive—and drew a pigskin case from my trouser pocket. There were several keys in the case and several other useful things as well, these last made of the finest German steel. I opened my case, knocked on the door for luck, and set to work.

A funny thing. The better your building, the higher your monthly rental, the more efficient your doorman, why, the easier it's going to be to crack your apartment. People who live in unattended walkups in Hell's Kitchen will fasten half a dozen deadbolt locks to their doors and add a Segal police lock for insurance. Tenement dwellers take it for granted that junkies will come to kick their doors in and strong-arm types will rip the cylinders out of their locks, so they make things as secure as they possibly can. But if the building itself is so set up as to intimidate your garden variety snatch-and-grab artist, then most tenants make do with the lock the landlord provides.

In this case the landlord provided a Rabson. Now there's nothing tacky about a Rabson lock. The Rabson is very good. But then so am I.

I suppose it took me a minute to open the lock. A minute may be long or short, significant or inconsequential. It is long indeed when you are spending it inserting burglar's tools into a lock of an apartment manifestly not your own, and when you know that during any of its sixty seconds another door down the hallway might open and some Nosey Parker might want to know just who you think you are and just what you think you are doing.

No one opened a door, no one got off the elevator. I did creative things with my finely tempered steel implements, and the tumblers tumbled and the lock mechanism turned and the deadbolt drew itself deliberately back and disengaged. When that happened I let out the breath I'd been holding and drew a fresh one. Then I wiggled my picks a little more and opened the spring lock, which was child's play after the deadbolt, and when it snicked back I felt that little surge of excitement that's always there when I open a lock. It's a little like a roller coaster ride and a little like sexual triumph, and you may make of all that what you will.

I turned the knob, eased the heavy door inward half an inch or so. My blood was really up now. You never know for certain what's going to be on the other side of the door. That's one of the things that makes it exciting, but it also makes it scary, and it's still scary no matter how many times you've done it.

Once the lock's open, though, you can't do it an inch at a time like an old lady slipping into a swimming pool. So I pushed the door open and went inside.

The room was dark. I closed the door behind me, turned the bolt, dug a penlight flash out of my pocket and played the beam around. The drapes were drawn. That explained the room's utter darkness, and it meant I might as well turn the lights on because no one could see in from the building across the street. Apartment 311 fronted on Sixty-seventh Street but with the drapes drawn it might as well have been fronting on a blank wall.

The wall switch near the door turned on a pair of table lamps with leaded glass Tiffany-type shades. They looked like reproductions to me but they were nice ones. I moved around the room, taking time to get the feel of it. I've always done this.

Nice room. Large, about fifteen by twenty-five feet. A highly polished dark oak floor with two oriental rugs on it. The larger one was Chinese and the smaller one at the far end of the room might have been a Bokhara, but I couldn't tell you for sure. I suppose I ought to know more about rugs but I've never taken the time to learn because they're too much trouble to steal.

Naturally I went over to the desk first. It was a nineteenth-century rolltop, oaken and massive, and I'd probably have been drawn to it simply because I like desks like that, but in this case my whole reason for being in this apartment was tucked away in one of its drawers or cubbyholes. That's what the shifty-eyed and pear-shaped man had told me, and who was I to doubt his word?

"There's this big old desk," he had said, aiming his chocolate eyes over my left shoulder. "What you call a rolltop. The top rolls up."

"Clever name for it," I'd said.

He had ignored this. "You'll see it the minute you walk in the room. Big old mother. He keeps the box in the desk." He moved his little hands about, to indicate the dimensions of the box we were discussing. "About like so. About the size of a box of cigars. Maybe a little bigger, maybe a little smaller. Basically I'd call it cigar-box size. Box is blue."

"Blue."

"Blue leather. Covered in leather. I suppose it's wood under the leather. Rather than being leather straight through. What's under the leather don't matter. What matters is what's inside the box."

"What's inside the box?"

"That don't matter." I stared at him, ready to ask him which of us was to be Abbott and which Costello. He frowned. "What's in the box for you," he said, "is five thousand dollars. Five kay for a few minutes' work. As to what's actually inside the box we're talking about, see, the box is locked."

"I see."

His eyes moved from the air above my left shoulder to the air above my right shoulder, pausing en route to flick contemptuously at my own eyes. "Locks," he said, "prolly don't mean too much to you."

"Locks mean a great deal to me."

"This lock, the lock on the box, you prolly shouldn't open it."

"I see."

"Be a very bad idea for you to open it. You bring me the box, you get the rest of your money, and everybody's happy."

"Oh," I said. "I see what you're doing."

"Huh?"

"You're *threatening* me," I said. "How curious."

The eyes widened but only for a moment. "Threats? Not for the world, kid. Advice and threats, there's a world of difference. I wouldn't dream of threatening you."

"Well, I wouldn't dream of opening your blue leather box."

"Leather-covered."

"Right."

"Not that it makes a difference."

"Hardly. What color blue?"

"Huh?"

"Dark blue, light blue, robin's egg blue, Prussian blue, cobalt blue, powder blue. What color?"

"What's the difference?"

"I wouldn't want to bring the wrong blue box."

"Don't worry about it, kid."

"If you say so."

"Just so it's a blue leather box. Unopened."

"Gotcha."

Since that conversation I'd been whiling away the hours trying to decide whether I'd open the box or not. I knew myself well enough to recognize that any lock constitutes an immediate temptation for me, and when I've been cautioned against opening a particular lock that only increases the attraction of it.

On the other hand, I'm not a kid anymore. When you've been

inside a couple of times your judgment is supposed to improve, and if it seemed likely that there was more danger than profit in opening the elusive blue box . . .

But before I came to terms with the question I had to find the box, and before I did that I had to open the desk, and I wasn't even ready to tackle that project yet. First I wanted to get the feel of the room.

Some burglars, like some lovers, just want to get in and get out. Others try to psych out the people they're thieving from, building up a whole mental profile of them out of what their houses reveal. I do something a little different. I have this habit of creating a life for myself to suit the surroundings I find myself in.

So I now took this apartment and transformed it from the residence of one J. Francis Flaxford to the sanctum sanctorum of yours truly, Bernard Grimes Rhodenbarr. I settled myself in an oversized wing chair upholstered in dark green leather, swung my feet up on the matching ottoman, and took a leisurely look at my new life.

Pictures on the walls, old oils in elaborate gilded frames. A little landscape that clearly owed a lot to Turner, although a lesser hand had just as clearly held the brush. A pair of old portraits in matching oval frames, a man and a woman eyeing each other thoughtfully over a small fireplace in which not a trace of ash reposed. Were they Flaxford's ancestors? Probably not, but did he attempt to pass them off as such?

No matter. I'd call them my ancestors, and make up outrageous stories about them. And there'd be a fire in the fireplace, casting a warm glow over the room. And I'd sit in this chair with a book and a glass, and perhaps a dog at my feet. A large dog, a large old dog, one not given to yaps or abrupt movements. Perhaps a stuffed dog might be best all around. . . .

Books. There was a floor lamp beside my chair, its bulb at reading height. The wall behind the chair was lined with bookshelves and another small case of books, one of those revolving stands, stood on the floor alongside the chair. On the other side of the chair was a lower table holding a silver cigarette dish and a massive cut-glass ashtray.

All right. I'd do a lot of reading here, and quality stuff, not modern junk. Perhaps those leather-bound sets were just there for show, their pages still uncut. Well, it would be a different story if I were living here. And I'd keep a decanter of good brandy on the table beside me. No, two decanters, a pair of those wide-bottomed ship's decanters, one filled with brandy, one with a vintage port. There'd be room for them when I got rid of the cigarette dish. The ashtray could stay. I liked the size and style of it, and I might want to take up smoking a pipe. Pipes had always burned my tongue in the past, but perhaps as I worked my way through the wisdom of the ages, feet up on the hassock, book in hand, port and brandy within easy reach, a fire glowing on the hearth . . .

I spent a few minutes on the fantasy, figuring out a little more about the life I'd lead in Mr. Flaxford's apartment. I suppose it's silly and childish to do this and I know it wastes time. But I think it serves a purpose. It gets rid of some tension. I get wired very tight when I'm in someone else's place. The fantasy makes the place my own home in a certain way, at least for the short time I'm inside it, and that seems to help. I'm not convinced that's why I started doing it in the first place, or why I've continued.

The time I wasted couldn't have amounted to very much, anyway, because I looked at my watch just before I put my gloves on to go to work and it was only seventeen minutes after nine. I use sheer skintight rubber gloves, the kind doctors wear, and I cut out circles on the palms and backs so my hands won't perspire as much. As with other skintight rubber things, you don't really lose all that much in the way of sensitivity and you make up for it in peace of mind.

The desk had two locks. One opened the rolltop and the other, in the top right-hand drawer, unlocked that drawer and all the others at once. I probably could have found the keys—most people stow desk keys very close to the desk itself—but it was faster and easier to open both locks with my own tools. I've never yet run into a desk lock that didn't turn out to be candy.

These two were no exception. I rolled up the rolltop and studied the usual infinite array of pigeonholes, tiny drawer upon tiny drawer, cubicle after cubicle. For some reason our ancestors found this an efficient system for the organization of one's business affairs. It's always seemed to me that it would have to be more trouble keeping track of what bit of trivia you stowed in what arcane hiding place than it would be to keep everything in a single steamer trunk and just rummage through it when there was something you needed. But I suppose there are plenty of people who get enormously turned on by the notion of a place for everything and everything in its place. They're the people who line up their shoes in the closet according to height. And they remember to rotate their tires every three months, and they set aside one day a week for clipping their fingernails.

And what do they do with the clippings? Stow 'em in a pigeonhole, I suppose.

The blue leather box wasn't under the rolltop, and my pear-shaped client had so positioned his little hands as to indicate a box far too large for any of the pigeonholes and little drawers, so

I opened the other lock and released the catches on all the lower drawers. I started with the top right drawer because that's where most people tend to put their most important possessions—I've no idea why—and I worked my way from drawer to drawer looking for a blue box and not finding one.

I went through the drawers quickly, but not too quickly. I wanted to get out of the apartment as soon as possible because that's always a good idea, but I had not committed myself to pass up any other goodies the apartment might contain. A great many people keep cash around the house, and others keep traveler's checks, and still others keep coin collections and readily salable jewelry and any number of interesting things which fit neatly enough into a Bloomingdale's shopping bag. I wanted the four thousand dollars due me upon delivery of the blue box—the thousand I'd received in advance bulged reassuringly in my hip pocket—but I also wanted whatever else might come my way. I was standing in the apartment of a man who did not evidently have to worry about the source of his next meal, and if I got lucky I might very well turn a five-thousand-dollar sure thing into a score big enough to buy my groceries for the next year or so.

Because I no longer like to work any more than I have to. It's a thrill, no question about it, but the more you work the worse the odds get. Crack enough doors and sooner or later you are going to fall down. Every once in a while you'll get arrested and a certain number of arrests will stick. Four, five, six jobs a year—that ought to be plenty. I didn't think so a few years ago when I still had things to prove to myself. Well, you live and you learn, and generally in that order.

I gave those drawers a fast shuffle, down one side and up the other, and I found papers and photograph albums and account ledgers and rings full of keys that probably didn't fit anything and a booklet half-full of three-cent stamps (remember them?) and one of a pair of fur-lined kid gloves and one of a pair of unlined pigskin gloves and one earmuff of the sort that your mother made you wear and a perpetual calendar issued in 1949 by the Marine Trust Company of Buffalo, New York, and a Bible, King James version, no larger than a pack of playing cards, and a pack of playing cards, Tally-Ho version, no larger than the Bible, and a lot of envelopes which probably still had letters in them, but who cared, and stacks of canceled checks bearing various dates over the past two decades, held together by desiccated rubber bands, and enough loose paper clips to make a chain that would serve as a jump rope for a child, or perhaps even for an adult, and a postcard from Watkins Glen, and some fountain pens and some ball pens and some felt pens and no end of pencils, all with broken tips, and . . .

And no coin collections, no cash, no traveler's checks, no bearer bonds, no stock certificates, no rings, no watches, no cut or uncut precious stones (although there was a rather nice chunk of petrified wood with felt glued to the bottom so it could be used as a paperweight), no gold bars, no silver ingots, no stamps more precious than the three-cent jobs in the booklet, and, by all the saints in heaven, no blue box, leather or otherwise.

Hell.

This didn't make me happy, but neither did it make me throw up. What it made me do was straighten up and sigh a little, and it made me wonder idly where old Flaxford kept the Scotch until I reminded myself that I never drink on a job, and it made me think about the cigarettes in the silver dish until I recalled that I'd given up the nasty things years ago. So I sighed again and got ready to give the drawers another look-see, because it's very easy to miss something when you're dealing with a desk that is such a reservoir of clutter, even something as substantial as a cigar box, and I looked at my watch and noted that it was twenty-three minutes of ten, and decided that I would really prefer to be on my way by ten, or ten thirty at the very latest. Once more through the desk, then, to be followed if necessary by a circuit of other logical hiding places in the living room, and then if need be a tour of the apartment's other rooms, however many there might be of them, and then adieu, adieu. And so I blew on my hands to cool them as they were beginning to sweat a bit, not that blowing on them did much good, encased in rubber gloves as they were, and this may well have led me to sigh a third time, and then I heard a key in the lock and froze.

The apartment's tenant, J. Francis Flaxford, was supposed to be off the premises until midnight at the very least.

By the same token, the blue box was supposed to be in the desk.

I stood facing the door, my hip braced against the desk. I listened as the key turned in the lock, easing back the deadbolt, then turning farther to draw back the spring lock. There was an instant of dead silence. Then the door flew inward and two boys in blue burst through it, guns in their hands, the muzzles trained on me.

"Easy," I said. "Relax. It's only me."

Chapter Two

THE first cop through the door was a stranger, and a very young and fresh-faced one at that. But I recognized his partner, a grizzled, gray chap with jowls and a paunch and a long sharp nose. His name was Ray Kirschmann and he'd been with the NYPD since the days when they carried muskets. He'd collared me a few years earlier and had proved to be a reasonable man at the time.

"Son of a gun," he said, lowering his own gun and putting a calming hand upon the gun of his young associate. "If it ain't Mrs. Rhodenbarr's son, Bernard. Put the heat away, Loren. Bernie here is a perfect gentleman."

Loren bolstered his gun and let out a few cubic feet of air. Burglars are not the only poor souls who tend to tense up when entering doors other than their own. And trust Ray to make sure his young partner cleared the threshold ahead of him.

I said, "Hi, Ray."

"Nice to see ya, Bernie. Say hello to my new partner, Loren Kramer. Loren, this here is Bernie Rhodenbarr."

We exchanged hellos and I extended a hand for a shake. This confused Loren, who looked at my hand and then began rumbling with the pair of handcuffs hanging from his gun belt.

Ray laughed. "For Chrissake," he said. "Nobody ever puts cuffs on Bernie. This ain't one of your mad dog punks, Loren. This is a professional burglar you got here."

"Oh."

"Close the door, Loren."

Loren closed the door—he didn't bother to turn the bolt—and I did a little more relaxing myself. We had thus far attracted no attention. No neighbors milled in the hallways. And so I had every intention of spending what remained of the night beneath my own good roof.

Politely I said, "I wasn't expecting you, Ray. Do you come here often?"

"You son of a gun, you." He grinned. "Gettin' sloppy in your old age, you know that? We're in the car and we catch a squeal, woman hears suspicious noises. And you was always quiet as a mouse. How old are you, Bernie?"

"Be thirty-five in April. Why?"

"Taurus?" This from Loren.

"The end of May. Gemini."

"My wife's a Taurus," Loren said. He had liberated his night-stick from its clip and was slapping it rhythmically against his palm.

"Why?" I asked again, and there was a moment of confusion with Loren trying to explain that his wife was a Taurus because of when she was born, and me explaining that what I wanted to know was why Ray had asked me my age, and Ray looking sorry he'd brought the whole thing up in the first place. There was something about Loren that seemed to generate confusion.

"Just age making you sloppy," Ray explained. "Making noises, drawing attention. It's not like you."

"I never made a sound."

"Until tonight."

"I'm talking about tonight. Anyway, I just got here."

"When?"

"I don't know, a few minutes ago. Maybe fifteen or twenty minutes at the outside. Ray? You sure you got the right apartment?"

"We got the one's got a burglar in it, don't we?"

"There's that," I admitted. "But did they specify this apartment? Three-eleven?"

"Not the number, but they said the right front apartment on the third floor. That's this one."

"A lot of people mix up left and right."

He looked at me, and Loren slapped the nightstick against his palm and managed to drop it. There was a leather thong attaching it to his belt but the thong was long enough so that the nightstick hit the floor. It bounced on the Chinese rug and Loren retrieved it while Ray glowered at him.

"That's more noise than I made all night," I said.

"Look, Bernie—"

"Maybe they meant the apartment above this one. Maybe the woman was English. They figure floors differently over there. They call the first floor the ground floor, see, so what they call the third floor would be the floor three flights up, which you and I would call the *fourth* floor, and—"

"Jesus."

I looked at Loren, then back at Ray again.

"What are you, crazy? You want me to read you your rights and all so you'll remember you're a criminal caught in the act? What the hell's got into you, Bernie?"

"It's just that I just got here. And I never made a sound."

"So maybe a cat knocked a plant off a shelf in the apartment next door and we just got lucky and came here by mistake. It's still you and us, right?"

"Right." I smiled what certainly ought to have been a rueful smile. "You got lucky, all right. I'm nice and fat tonight."

"That so?"

"Very fat."

"Interesting," Ray said.

"You got the key from the doorman?"

"Uh-huh. He wanted to come up and let us in but we told him he ought to stay at his post."

"So nobody actually knows I'm here but you two."

The two of them looked at each other. They were a nice contrast, Ray in his lived-in uniform, Loren all young and neat and freshly laundered. "That's true," Ray said. "Far as it goes."

"Oh?"

"This'd be a very good collar for us. Me'n Loren, we could use a good collar. Might get a commendation out of it."

"Oh, come on," I said.

"Always possible."

"The hell it is. You didn't nail me on your own initiative. You followed up a radio squawk. Nobody's going to pin a medal on you."

"Well, you got a point there," Ray said. "What do you think, Loren?"

"Well," Loren said, slapping the stick against his palm and nibbling thoughtfully on his lower lip. The stick was beat up and scratched in contrast to the rest of his outfit. I had the feeling he dropped it often, and on surfaces more abrasive than Chinese carpets.

"How fat are you, Bernie?"

I didn't see any point in haggling. I generally carry an even thousand dollars in walkaway money, and that was what I had now. Coincidentally enough, the ten hundreds in my left hip pocket were the very ones I'd taken as an advance on the night's work, so if I gave it all to my coppish friends I'd break even, with nothing lost but my cab fare and a couple of hours of my time. My shifty-eyed friend would be out a thousand dollars but that was his hard luck and he would just have to write it off.

"A thousand dollars," I said.

I watched Ray Kirschmann's face. He considered trying for more but must have decided I'd gone straight to the top. And there was no dodging the fact that it was a satisfactory score since it only had to be cut two ways.

"That's fat," he admitted. "On your person right now?"

I took out the money and handed it to him. He fanned the bills and gave them a count with his eyes, trying not to be too obvious about it.

"You pick up anything in here, Bernie? Because if we was to report there was nobody here and then the tenant calls in a burglary complaint, we don't look too good."

I shrugged. "You could always claim I left before you got here," I told him, "but you won't have to. I couldn't find anything worth stealing, Ray. I just got here and all I touched is the desk."

"We could frisk him," Loren suggested. Ray and I both gave

him a look and he turned a deeper pink than his usual shade. "It was just a thought," he said.

I asked him what sign he was.

"Virgo," he said.

"Should go well with Taurus."

"Both earth signs," he said. "Lots of stability."

"I would think so."

"You interested in astrology?"

"Not particularly."

"I think there's a lot to be said for it. Ray's a Sagittarius."

"Jesus Christ," Ray said. He looked at the bills again, gave a small shrug, then folded them once and found them a home in his pocket. Loren watched this procedure somewhat wistfully. He knew he'd get his share later, but still . . .

Ray gnawed a fingernail. "How'd you get in, Bernie? Fire escape?"

"Front door."

"Right past the clown downstairs? They're terrific, these doormen."

"Well, it's a large building."

"Not that large. Still, you do look the part. That clean-cut East Side look and those clothes." I live on the West Side myself, and usually wear jeans. "And I suppose you carried a briefcase, right?"

"Not exactly." I pointed to my Bloomie's bag. "That."

"Even better. Well, I guess you can pick it up and walk right out again. Wait a minute." He frowned. "*We'll* leave first. I like it better that way. Otherwise, why are we taking so much time here, et cetera, and et cetera. But don't get light-fingered after we split, huh?"

"There's nothing here to take," I said.

"I want your word on it, Bernie."

I avoided laughing. "You've got it," I said solemnly.

"Give us three minutes and then go straight out. But don't hang around no more'n that, Bernie."

"I won't."

"Well," he said. He turned and reached for the door, and then Loren Kramer said he had to go to the bathroom. "Jesus Christ," Ray said.

Loren said, "Bernie? Where is it, do you know?"

"Search me," I said. "Not literally."

"Huh?"

"I never got past this desk," I said. "I suppose the john must be back there somewhere."

Loren went looking for it while Ray stood there shaking his head. I asked him how long Loren had been his partner. "Too long," he said.

"I know what you mean."

"He ain't a bad kid, Bernie."

"Seems nice enough."

"But he's so damn stupid. And the astrology drives me straight up the wall. You figure there's anything in that crap?"

"Probably."

"But even so, who gives a shit, right? Who cares if his wife's a Taurus? She's a good-looking bitch, I'll give her that much. But Loren, shit, he was ready to search you. Just now when you said 'Search me.' The putz woulda done it."

"I had that feeling."

"The one good thing, he's reasonable. They gave me this straight arrow a while back and you couldn't do nothing with him. I mean he even paid for his coffee. At least Loren, when somebody puts money in his hand he knows to close his fist around it."

"Thank God for that."

"That's what I say. If anything, he likes the bread too much, but I guess his wife is good at spending it fast as he brings it home. You figure it's on account of she's a Taurus?"

"You'd have to ask Loren."

"He might tell me. But you can put up with a lot of stupidity in exchange for a little reasonableness, I have to say that for him. Just so he don't kill hisself with that nightstick of his, bouncing it off his knee or something. Bernie? Take the gloves off."

"Huh?"

"The rubber gloves. You don't want to wear those on the street."

"Oh," I said, and stripped them off. Somewhere in the inner recesses of the apartment Loren coughed and bumped into something. I stuffed my gloves into my pocket. "All the tools of the trade," Ray said. "Jesus, I'd always rather deal with pros, guys like you. Like even if we had to bag you tonight. Say I had the doorman backing my play and there was no way to cool it off. No money in it that way but at least I'm dealing with a professional."

Somewhere a toilet flushed. I resisted an impulse to look at my watch.

"You feel comfortable about it," he went on. "Know what I mean? Like tonight, coming through that door. I didn't know what we was gonna find on the other side of it."

"I know the feeling," I assured him, and started to reach for my shopping bag. I caught a glimpse of Ray's face that made me turn to see what he was staring at, and what he was staring at was

Loren at the far end of the room with a mouth as wide as the Holland Tunnel and a face as white as a surgical mask.

"In . . . " he said. "In . . . In . . . In the bedroom!" And then, all in a rush: "Coming back from the toilet and I turned the wrong way and there's the bedroom and this guy, he's dead, this dead guy, head beaten in and there's blood all over the place, warm blood, the guy's still warm, you never saw anything like it, Jesus, I knew it, you can never trust a Gemini, I knew it, they lie all the time, oh God—"

And he flopped on the rug. The one that may very well have been a Bokhara.

And Ray and I looked at each other.

Talk about professionalism. We both went promptly insane. He just stood there with his face looming, not going for his gun, not reaching for me, not even moving, just standing flatfooted like the flatfoot he indisputably was. And I, on the other hand, began behaving wholly out of character, in a manner neither of us ever expected I might be capable of.

I sprang at him. He went on gaping at me, too astonished even to react, and I barreled into him and sent him sprawling and bolted without waiting to see where he landed. I shot out the door and found the stairs right where I'd left them, and I raced down two flights and dashed through the lobby at the very pace the word *breakneck* was coined to describe.

The doorman, obliging as ever, held the door for me. "I'll take care of you at Christmas!" I sang out. And scurried off without even waiting for a reply.

Chapter Three

IT's a good thing the sidewalks were fairly clear. Otherwise I probably would have run straight into somebody. As it was, I managed to reach the corner with a simple stretch of broken-field running, and by the time I took a left at Second Avenue, logic and shortness of breath combined to take the edge off my panic. No one seemed to be pelting down the street behind me. I slowed to a rapid walk. Even in New York people tend to stare at you if you run. It may not occur to them to do anything about it, but it gets on my nerves when people stare at me.

After a block and a half of rapid walking I stuck out a hand and attracted the attention of a southbound cab. I gave him my address and he turned a couple of corners to transform himself into a northbound cab, but by that time I'd changed my mind. My apartment was nestled high atop a relatively new high-rise at West End and Seventy-first, and on a clear day (which comes up now and then) you can see, if not forever, at least the World

Trade Center and selected parts of New Jersey. And it's a perfect refuge from the cares of the city, not to mention the slings and arrows of outrageous fortune, which is why I automatically spoke the address to the driver.

But it was also the first place Ray Kirschmann and his fellows would come looking for me. All they had to do was check the phone book, for God's sake.

I pressed myself back into my seat and patted my left breast pocket in a reflexive hunt for the pack of cigarettes that hadn't been there in several years. If I lived in that apartment on East Sixty-seventh, I thought, I could sit in the green leather chair and knock dottle from my pipe into the cut-glass ashtray. But as things stood . . .

Relax, Bernard. Think!

There were several things to think about. Like, just who had invested a thousand dollars in setting me up for a murder charge, and just why the oddly familiar pear-shaped man had chosen me for the role of imbecile. But I didn't really have time for that sort of long-range thinking. I'd gotten a break—one cop collapsing in a providential faint, the other reacting slowly even as I was reacting with uncharacteristic speed. That break had given me a head start, but the head start probably didn't amount to more than a handful of minutes. It could vanish before I knew it.

I had to go to ground. Had to find a bolt hole. I'd shaken the hounds from my trail for a moment or two and it was up to me to regain the safety of my burrow before they recaptured the scent. (It didn't thrill me that all the phrases that came to me were from the language of fox hunting, incidentally.)

I shrugged off the thought and tried to get specific. My own apartment was out; it would be full of cops within the hour. I needed a place to go, some safe and sound place with four walls and a ceiling and a floor, all of them reasonably close together. It had to be a place that no one would think to connect with me and one where I could not be readily discovered or observed. And it had to be in New York, because I'd be a lot easier to run down once I was off my home ground.

A friend's apartment.

The cab cruised northward while I reviewed my list of friends and acquaintances and established that there was not a single one of them whom I could drop in on. (In on whom I could drop? No matter.) My problem, you see, was that I had always tended to avoid bad company. Outside of prison—and I prefer to be outside of prison as often as possible—I never associate with other burglars, hold-up men, con artists, swindlers or miscellaneous thieves and grifters. When one is within stone walls one's ability to pick and choose is circumscribed, certainly, but on the outside I limit myself to people who are, if not strictly honest, at least not the felonious sort. My boon companions may pilfer office supplies from their employers, fabricate income tax deductions out of the whole cloth, file parking tickets in the incinerator, and bend various commandments perilously close to the breaking point. But they are none of them jailbirds, at least as far as I know, and as far as they know neither am I.

It should consequently not surprise you to learn that I have no particularly close friends. With none of them knowing the full truth about me, no intimacy has ever really developed. There are chaps I play chess with and chaps I play poker with. There are a couple of lads with whom I'll take in a fight or a ball game. There are women with whom I dine, women with whom I may see a play or hear a concert, and with some of these ladies fair I'll now and then share a pillow. But it's been quite a while since there was a male companion in my life whom I'd call a real friend, and almost as long since I'd been involved with a woman on more than a casual basis. That modern disease of detachment, I suppose, augmented by the solitary nature of the secretive burglar.

I'd never had occasion to regret all of this before, except on those once-in-a-while bad nights everybody has when your own company is the worst company in the world and there's nobody you know well enough to call at three in the morning. Now, though, what it all meant was there was no one on earth I could ask to hide me. And if there was it wouldn't help, because if I had a close friend or a lover that's the first place the cops would look, and they'd be on the doorstep an hour or two after I was through the door.

Problems . . .

"You want me to turn around?"

My driver's voice shook me out of my reverie. He had pulled to a stop and had turned around to blink at me through the Plexiglas partition that kept him safe from homicidal fares. "Senny-first 'n' Wes' End," he announced. "You want this side or the other?" I blinked back, turned up my coat collar, shrank down inside it like a startled turtle. "Mac," he said patiently, "want I should turn around?"

"By all means," I said.

"That means yes?"

"That means yes."

He waited while traffic cleared, then arched the cab in the traditional illegal U-turn, braking smoothly to a stop in front of my very own building. Could I spare a minute to duck inside, grab some clothes and my case money, be out in no time at all. . . .

No.

His hand reached to throw the flag shutting off the meter. "Hold it," I said. "Now drive downtown."

His hand hovered over the flag like a hummingbird over a flower. Then he withdrew it and turned again to look querulously at me. "Drive downtown?"

"Right."

"You don't like this place no more?"

"It's not as I remembered it."

His eyes took on that wary New York look of a man who realizes he's dealing with a lunatic. "I guess," he said.

"Nothing's the same anymore," I said recklessly. "The neighborhood's gone to hell."

"Jesus," he said, cab in motion now, driver at ease. "Lemme tell you, this here is nothin'. You oughta see where I live. That's up in the Bronx. I don't know if you're familiar with the Bronx. But you're talking about a neighborhood on the skids—"

And talk about a neighborhood on the skids is precisely what he did, and he did it all the way down the western edge of Manhattan. The best thing about the conversation was its utter predictability. I didn't have to listen to it. I just let my mind go wherever it wanted while my mouth filled in with the appropriate grunts and uh-huhs and izzatsos as the occasion demanded.

So I sent my mind on a tour of my friends, such as they were. The wood pushers I whipped routinely at chess, the card sharps who just as routinely trimmed me at poker. The sports fans. The drinking companions. The disconcertingly short list of young ladies with whom I'd been lately keeping the most cursory sort of company.

Rodney Hart.

Rodney Hart!

His name popped into my mind like a fly ball into shallow right field. A tall fellow, spare of flesh, with high and prominent eyebrows and a longish nose, the nostrils of which tended to flare when he was holding anything much better than two pair. I'd first met him at a poker game perhaps a year and a half ago, and since then I'd seen him precisely two times away from the card table—once in a Village bar when we happened to run into each other and chatted our way through a couple of beers, and another time when he had the second lead in a short-lived off-Broadway show and I went backstage after the performance with a young lady I was trying to impress. (It didn't work.)

Good old Rodney Hart!

What, you may well ask, was so wonderful about Rodney? Well, in the first place, I happened to know that he lived alone. More important, he wasn't home now and wouldn't be back in town for a couple of months. Just the other week or so he'd turned up at the poker game and announced we wouldn't have him to kick around anymore. He'd just signed for the road company of *Two If By Sea* and would be traveling the length and breadth of these United States, bringing Broadway's idea of culture to the provinces. And he'd even dropped the gratuitous information that he wasn't subletting his apartment. "Not worth it," he'd said. "I've had the place for years and I pay a hot ninety a month in rent. The landlord doesn't even bother getting increases he's entitled to. He likes renting to actors, if you can believe it. The roar of the greasepaint and all that. He eats it up. Anyway, it's worth ninety a month not to have some sonofabitch sitting on my toilet and sleeping in my bed."

Ha!

He didn't know it, but the sonofabitch who would be sitting on his potty seat and lolling between his percales was none other than Bernard Rhodenbarr. And I wouldn't even pay him ninety a month for the privilege.

But where the hell did he live?

I seemed to remember that he lived in the Village somewhere, and I decided that was as much as I had to know while I was in this particular cab. Because I had unquestionably made myself a memorable passenger, and the papers would shortly be full of my face, and the driver might, for the first time in his unhappy life, actually go so far as to put two and two together.

"Right here is fine," I said.

"Here?"

We were somewhere on Seventh Avenue now, a couple of blocks from Sheridan Square. "Just stop the cab," I said.

"You're the boss," the driver said, using a phrase which has always seemed to me to be the politest possible way of expressing absolute contempt. I dug out my wallet, paid the man, gave him a tip designed to justify his contempt, and while so doing began to regret bitterly the thousand dollars I'd paid to Ray and Loren. Hardly the best investment I had ever made. If I had that thousand now it might give me a certain degree of mobility. But all I had, after squaring things with the cabbie, was seventy dollars and change. And it seemed somehow unlikely that Rod would be the sort to leave substantial quantities of cash around his empty apartment.

And where was that apartment, anyway?

I found that answer in a phone booth, thinking as I turned the directory how providential it was that Rod was an actor. It seems as though everyone else I know has an unlisted number, but actors are another breed; they do everything but write their numbers on lavatory walls. (And some of them do that.) Good old Rod was listed, of course, and while Hart is a reasonably common name Rodney is reasonably uncommon, and there he was, praise be to God, with an apartment on Bethune Street deep in the bowels of the West Village. A quiet street, an out-of-the-way street, a street the tourists never trod. What could be better?

The book gave not only his address but his phone number as well, as telephone books are wont to do, and I invested a dime and dialed the number. (One does this sort of thing before breaking and entering.) It rang seven times, which I thought was probably enough, but I'm compulsive; I always let phones in potentially burglarable apartments go through a tedious twelve rings. But this one rang only seven before someone picked it up, at which point I came perilously close to vomiting.

"Seven-four-one-nine," a soft female voice said, and my risen gorge sank and I calmed down. Because just as actors have listed phones so do they have services to answer them, and that was what this voice represented; the number which had been spoken to me was nothing other than the last four digits of Rodney's phone number. I cleared my throat and asked when Rodney would be back in town, and the lady with the dulcet tones obligingly informed me that he would be on tour for another fifteen weeks, that he was in St. Louis at the moment, and that she could supply me with the number of his hotel there if I wished. I didn't wish. I suppressed an infantile urge to leave a comic message and returned the phone to its cradle.

It took a little doing but I managed to find Bethune Street and walked west on it until I located Rod's building. It was half a block west of Washington Street in a neighborhood that was half brownstones and the other half warehouses. The building I wanted was a poor but honest five-story brownstone indistinguishable from its neighbors on either side but for the rusty numerals alongside the front door. I stayed on the street a moment to make sure there was no one taking obvious notice of me, then slipped into the front vestibule. I scanned the row of buttons on the wall, looking for names of illustrious actors and actresses, but Helen Hayes wasn't listed and neither were the Lunts. Rod was, however; one R. Hart was inked in as occupying Apartment 5-R. Since there were five floors and two apartments to a floor, that meant he was on the top floor at the rear of the building, and what could be less obtrusive than that?

Because old habits die hard, I gave his bell a good ringing and waited for anyone who might be in his apartment to buzz me back. Happily no one did. I then thought of ringing other bells at random. This is what I would do on a job. People buzz you on through the locked front door without a qualm, and if they happen to pop out into the hallway to see who you are you just smile apologetically and say that you forgot your key. Works like a charm. But Rod lived on the top floor, which meant I'd have to walk past all the other floors, and anyone who noticed me might notice again when the papers saw fit to print my picture, and I might be holed up here for a while, if not forever, and . . .

Didn't seem worth the risk, small though the risk might be. Especially since it took me less than fifteen seconds to let myself through that front door. A strong wind could have opened that lock.

I scampered up four flights to the top floor and took deep breaths until my heartbeat returned to normal. Rod's door had 5-R on it and I went and stood in front of it and listened. The door at the other end of the hallway, 5-F, had no light shining underneath it. I knocked on Rod's door and waited, and knocked again, and then I took out my burglar's tools.

Rod had three locks on his door. Sometime in the past an amateur had dug at the frame around one of them with a chisel or screwdriver, but it didn't look as though he'd accomplished anything. Rod's locks included a fancy Medeco cylinder, a Segal police lock with a steel bar wedged against the door from within, and a cheap piece of junk that was just there for nuisance value. I knocked off the third lock first to get it out of the way, then tackled the Segal. It's good insurance against a junkie kicking the door in and it's not easy to pick but I had the tools and the touch and it didn't keep me waiting long. The tumblers fell into place and the steel bar slid aside in its channel and that left the Medeco.

The Medeco's the one they advertise as pickproof and of course that's errant nonsense, there is no such thing, but it's a pardonable exaggeration. What it meant was that I had to do two jobs at once. Suppose you're a cryptographer and you're given a message which was encoded from an original in Serbo-Croat, a language you don't happen to speak. Now you have to crack the cypher and learn the language at the same time. That's not exactly what I had to do with the Medeco but it's as close an explanation as I can give you.

It was tricky and I made some mistakes. At one point I heard a door open and I almost had a seizure but the door was on the floor below and I relaxed again. Sort of. Then I tried again and screwed up again, and then I just plain hit it right and the message turned out to be "Open sesame." I popped inside and locked all three locks, just like the old maid in all the stories.

The first thing I did was walk through the whole apartment and make sure there weren't any bodies in it but my own. This wasn't that much of a chore. There was one large room with a bookcase set up as a sort of room divider screening off a sleeping alcove. The kitchen was small and uninviting. The bathroom was smaller and less inviting, and roaches scampered when I turned the light on. I turned it off again and went back to the living room.

A homey place, I decided. Well-worn furniture, probably purchased secondhand, but it was all comfortable enough. A scattering of plants, palms and philodendrons and others whose names I did not know. Posters on the walls, not pop posters of Bogart and Che but the sort printed to herald gallery openings, Miró and Chagall and a few others as unknown to me as some of the plants. I decided, all in all, that Rod had fairly good taste for an actor.

The rug was a ratty maroon carpet remnant about twelve feet square, its binding coming loose on one side and entirely absent on another, its threads quite bare in spots and patches, its overall appearance decidedly unwholesome. Next time, I thought, I'll bring along the bloody Bokhara.

And then I started to shake.

The Bokhara wasn't bloody, of course. Loren had merely fainted upon it. But the rug, in the bedroom I had not seen, presumably was. Bloody, that is.

Who had killed the man in the bedroom? For that matter, who was the man in the bedroom? J. Francis Flaxford himself? According to my information he was supposed to be away from home from eight thirty at the latest to midnight at the earliest. But if the whole point of that information had been to put me on the spot where I could get tagged for homicide, well, I couldn't really put too much stock in it.

35

A man. Dead. In the bedroom. And someone had beaten his head in, and he was still warm to the touch.

Terrific.

If I'd only had the sense to give the whole apartment a look-see the minute I went into it, then it would have been an entirely different story. One quick reconnaissance mission and I'd have seen the late lamented and been on my way. By the time the illustrious team of Kirschmann and Kramer made their entrance I'd have been back in my own little tower of steel and glass, sipping Scotch and smiling southward at the World Trade Center. Instead I was a fugitive from what passes for justice these days, the very obvious murderer of a murderee I'd never even met in the first place. And, because my presence of mind had been conspicuous by its absence, I'd reacted to things by (a) using brute force and (b) scramming. So that if there'd ever been any chance of convincing people I'd never killed anything more biologically advanced than cockroaches and mosquitoes, that chance had vanished without a trace.

I paced. I opened cupboards looking for liquor and found none. I went back, tested another chair, decided the one I'd already sat in was more comfortable, then rejected both chairs and stretched out on the couch.

And thought about the curious little man who'd gotten me into this mess in the first place.

Chapter Four

He was a thick-bodied man built rather like a bloated bowling pin. While he wasn't terribly stout, they'd been out of waists when he reached the front of the line that day. He must have had to guess where to put his belt each morning.

His face was round and jowly, with most of its features generally subdued. His eyes came closer to prominence than anything else. They were large and watchful and put me in mind of a pair of Hershey's Chocolate Kisses. (With the foil removed.) They were just that shade of brown. His hair was flat black and perfectly straight and he was balding in the middle, his hairline receding almost to the top of his skull. I suppose he was in his late forties. It's good I'm a burglar; I could never make a living guessing age and weight at a carnival.

I first met him on a Thursday night in a drinking establishment called The Watering Whole. (I'm sure whoever named it took great pride in his accomplishment.) The Whole, which in this instance is rather less than the sum of its parts, is a singles joint on Second Avenue in the Seventies, and unless you own a piece of it and want to inspect the register receipts there's really only one reason to go there. I had gone for that very reason, but that evening the selection of the accessible young ladies was as dazzling as the dinner menu on a lifeboat. I'd decided to move on as soon as my wineglass was empty when a voice at my elbow spoke my last name softly.

There was something faintly familiar about the voice. I turned, and there was the man I've described, his eyes just failing to meet my own. My first thought was that no, he was not a cop, and for this fact I was grateful. My second thought was that his face, like his voice, was familiar. My third thought was that I didn't know him. I don't recall my fourth thought, though it's possible I had one.

"Want to talk to you," he said. "Something you'll be interested in."

"We can talk here," I said. "Do I know you?"

"No. I guess we can talk here at that. Not much of a crowd, is there? I guess they do better on weekends."

"Generally," I said, and because it was that sort of a place, "Do you come here often?"

"First time."

"Interesting. I don't come here too often myself. Maybe once or twice a month. But it's interesting that we should run into each other here, especially since you seem to know me and I don't seem to know you. There's something familiar about you, and yet—"

"I followed you."

"I beg your pardon?"

"We coulda talked in your neighborhood, one of those joints on Seventy-second where you hang out, but I figure the man's gotta live there. You follow me? Why shit where the man eats, that's the question I ask myself."

"Ah," I said, as if that cleared things up.

Which it emphatically did not. You doubtless understand, having come into all this in roundabout fashion, but I had not the slightest idea what this man wanted. Then the bartender materialized before us and I learned that what my companion wanted was a tall Scotch and soda, and after that drink had been brought and my own wineglass replenished I learned what else he wanted.

"I want you to get something for me," he said.

"I don't understand."

"See, I know who you are, Rhodenbarr."

"So it would seem. At least you know my name, and I don't know yours, and—"

"I know how you make your money. Not to beat against the bush, Rhodenbarr, but what you are is a burglar."

I glanced nervously around the room. His voice had been pitched low and the conversational level in the bar was high, but his tone had about it the quality of a stage whisper and I checked to see if our conversation had caught anyone's interest. Apparently it had not.

I said, "Of course I don't know what you're talking about."

"I suggest you cut the shit."

"Oh," I said, and took a sip of wine. "All right. Consider it cut."

"There's this thing I want you to steal for me. It's in a certain apartment and I'll be able to tell you when you can get in. The building's got security, meaning a doorman around the clock, but there's no alarm system or nothing. Just the doorman."

"That's easy," I said, responding automatically. Then I gave my shoulders a shake-shake-shake. "You seem to know things about me," I said.

"Like what you do for a living."

"Yes, just that sort of thing. You should also know that I work alone."

"I didn't figure to go in there with you, kid."

"And that I find my own jobs."

He frowned. "What I'm doing is handing you a piece of cake, Rhodenbarr. I'm talking about you work an hour and you pick up five thousand dollars. That's not bad for an hour's work."

"Not bad at all."

"You do that forty hours a week, just go and figure the money you'd make."

"Two hundred thousand a week," I said promptly.

"Whatever the hell it comes to."

"That's what it comes to, all right. Annually, let me think now, annually that would come to ten million dollars a year. That's with two weeks off in the summer."

"Whatever."

"Or a week in the summer and a week in the winter. That's probably the best way to do it. Or I could take my vacation in the spring and fall to avail myself of low off-season rates. Though I suppose the savings wouldn't be significant if I was earning ten million dollars a year. Hell, I'd probably start blowing the bucks left and right. Flying first class. Taking cabs all the time. Buying the Mondavi zinfandel by the case instead of a niggling bottle at a time, and of course you save ten percent by the case but it's not a true savings because you always find yourself drinking more than you would otherwise. You've probably noticed that yourself. Of course the pressure might get to me, anyway, but then I'd have those two weeks of vacation to let it all out, and—"

"Funny," he said.

"Just nerves."

"If you say so. You done talking for a minute? I want you to do this thing for me. There's something I need and it's a cinch for you to get it for me. And my price is fair, don't you think?"

"That depends on what you want me to steal. If it's a diamond necklace worth a quarter of a million dollars, then I'd have to say five thousand is coolie's wages."

His face moved into what I suppose was meant as a smile. It failed to light up the room. "No diamond necklace," he said.

"Fine."

"What you'll get for me is worth five grand to me. It's not worth nothing to nobody else."

"What is it?"

"A box," he said, and described it, but I've told you that part already. "I'll give you the location, the apartment, everything, and for you it's like picking up candy in the street."

"I never pick up candy in the street."

"Huh?"

"Germs."

He waved the thought away with one of his little hands. "You know what I mean," he said. "No more jokes, huh?"

"Why don't you get it yourself?" He looked at me. "You know the apartment, the layout, everything. You even know what you're looking for, which is more than I know and more than I want to know. Why don't you keep the five thousand in your pocket?"

"And pull the job myself?"

"Why not?"

He shook his head. "Certain things I don't do," he said. "I don't take out my own appendix, I don't cut my own hair, I don't fix my own plumbing. Important things, things that need an expert's touch, what I do is I go and find an expert."

"And I'm your expert?"

"Right. You go through locks like grease through a goose. Or so I'm told."

"Who told you?"

An elaborate shrug. "You just never remember where you hear a thing these days," he said.

"I always remember."

"Funny," he said. "I never do. I got a memory with holes in it you could fall through." He touched my arm. "Place is filling up. What do you say we take our business outside. We'll walk up and down the street, we'll work everything out."

So we walked up and down the street, and though we didn't pick up any candy we did work everything out. We settled our terms and established that I would keep my schedule flexible for the next week or so. It wouldn't go more than that, he assured me.

He said, "I'll be in touch, Rhodenbarr. Next time I see you I'll give you the address and the time and everything you gotta know. Plus I'll have your thousand in front."

"I sort of thought you might let me have that now."

"Haven't got it on me. You never want to carry heavy cash on the street at night. All these muggers, these junkies."

"The streets aren't safe."

"It's a jungle."

"You could let me have the address now," I suggested. "And the name of the man who won't be home when I crack his crib. Give me that much time to check things out."

"You'll have all the time you need."

"I just thought—"

"Anyway, I don't happen to have the name or address at the moment. I told you about my memory, didn't I?"

"Did you?"

"I coulda sworn I did."

I shrugged. "It must have slipped my mind."

LATER that night I spent some time wondering why I'd agreed to do the job. I decided I had two motives. The money was first, and it was certainly not trivial. The certainty of five thousand dollars, plus the security of having the job already cased, outweighed the two-in-the-bush of setting up a job cold and then having to haggle with a fence.

But there was more to it than money. Something about my shmoo-shaped friend suggested that it would be unwise to refuse him. It's not that there was anything in particular I feared would happen to me if I told him to go roll his hoop. It just seemed unlikely to be a good idea.

And then there was curiosity. Who the hell was he? If I didn't know him, why did he seem so damned familiar? More important, how did he know about me? And what was his little game all about in the first place? If he was a pro, recognizing me as another pro, why were we circling each other like tropical birds in an involved mating ritual? I didn't necessarily expect ever to learn the answers to all these questions, but I felt they might turn up if I saw the thing through, and I didn't have any other work I was dying to do, and the money I had in reserve wouldn't last forever, and . . .

There's a luncheonette I go to once or twice a month on Amsterdam Avenue between Seventy-fourth and Seventy-fifth. The owner is a Turk with an intimidating moustache and the food he serves is every bit as Turkish, if less intimidating. I was sitting at the counter two days after my first meeting with my newfound friend. I'd just finished polishing off an exceptional bowl of lentil soup, and while I waited for my stuffed grape leaves I glanced at a selection of meerschaum pipes in a glass case on the wall. The man with the moustache goes home to Turkey every spring and returns with a satchel full of pipes, which he insists are better than anything you can buy over the counter at Dunhill's. I don't smoke a pipe so I'm not really tempted, but whenever I eat there I look at the pipes and try to figure out if there's a pipe smoker on earth I'm a close enough friend to so that I can buy him one of these beauties. There never is.

"My old man used to smoke a meerschaum," said a familiar voice beside me. "Only pipe he owned and he musta smoked it five, six times a day. Over the years the thing turned as black as the deuce of spades. He had this special glove he always wore when he smoked it. Just on the one hand, the hand he held the pipe in. He'd always sit in the same chair and just smoke that pipe real slow and easy. Had a special fitted case he kept it in when he wasn't smoking it. Case was lined in blue velvet."

"You do turn up at odd times."

"Then one day it broke," he went on. "I don't know whether he dropped it or set it down hard or it just got too old or whatever the hell happened. My memory, you know."

"Like a sieve."

"The worst. What's funny, the old man never got hisself a new pipe. Not a meerschaum, not a briar, not anything. Just quit the habit like it was no habit at all. When I think about it what I always come up with is he just never believed anything would happen to that pipe, and then when it did he realized that nothing on earth lasts forever, and if that was the case he figured the hell with it and he wouldn't smoke anymore. And he didn't."

"There's a reason you're telling me this story."

"No reason at all. Just that it came to mind looking at those pipes there. I don't want to interrupt your meal, Rhodenbarr."

"One might say you've already done that."

"So I'll be on the corner gettin' my shoes shined. I don't guess you'll be too long, will you?"

"I guess not."

He left. I ate my grape leaves. I hadn't intended to have dessert but I decided the hell with it and ate a small piece of too-sweet baklava and sipped a thick cup of inky Turkish coffee. I thought about having a second cup but figured it would keep me awake for four years and I didn't want that. So I paid the man with the moustache and walked to the shoeshine stand on the corner.

My friend told me everything I'd always wanted to know about J. Francis Flaxford and his blue leather box. If anything, he told me more than I wanted to know without answering any of my more important questions.

At one point I asked him his own name. He slid his soft brown eyes across my forehead and treated me to a look of infinite disappointment.

"Now I could tell you a name," he said, "but then what would you know that you don't know now? Not too much chance that it would be a real name, is there?"

"Not too much, no."

"So why should we make complications for ourselves? All you got to know is where and when to get the box, which we just went over, and how and where to give it to me so you can get the other four grand."

"You mean we'll plan that in advance? I thought I'd just go about my business and one of these days you'd turn up breathing over my shoulder at the delicatessen. Or maybe you'd be in the basement laundry room when I went down to throw my socks in the dryer."

He sighed. "You'll be inside Flaxford's place nine, nine thirty. You'll be outta there by eleven, eleven thirty the latest. Can't take too long to take a box out of a desk. You'll want to go home, have a drink, take a shower, change your clothes, that kind of thing." And drop off burglar tools and such, along with whatever sundry swag I might happen to acquire. "So you take yourself some time, and then what you do, you go to a place nice and convenient to your apartment. There's a bar on Broadway and I think it's Sixty-fourth Street, called Pandora's. You know it?"

"I've passed it."

"Nice quiet place. Get there, say, twelve thirty and take a booth at the back. There's no waitress so what you do is you get your drink at the bar and carry it back to your table."

"Sounds as though I'd better wear a suit."

"It's private and it's quiet and they leave you alone. You'll get there at twelve thirty and you might have to sit there half an hour."

"And then you'll turn up around one?"

"Right. Any problem, you wait until half past one and then you take the box and go home. But there won't be no problems."

"Of course not," I agreed. "But suppose someone tries to take the box away from me?"

"Well, take cabs, for Chrissake. You don't want to walk around at that hour. Oh, wait a minute."

I didn't say anything.

"You think I'd knock you over for a lousy four thousand dollars? Why would I do that?"

"Because it might be cheaper than paying me."

"Jesus," he said. "Then how could I use you some other time? Look, carry some heat if it's gonna make you feel better. Except all you do then is get nervous and shoot your own foot off. I swear you got nothing to worry about from me. You bring me the box and you get your four gees."

"Gees," I said.

"Huh?"

"Thou, kay, gees. Grand."

"Huh?"

"Four big ones."

"What's the point?"

"You've got so many nicknames for money, that's all. You're like a thesaurus of slang."

"Something wrong with the way I talk, Rhodenbarr?"

"No," I said. "Nothing. It's just me. My nerves, I guess. I get all keyed up."

"Yeah," he said thoughtfully. "I just bet you do."

AND now I sat up on Rod's couch and looked at my watch. It was getting on for midnight. I'd gotten out of the Flaxford apartment with plenty of time to spare, but all the same it didn't look as though I'd be in Pandora's by twelve thirty. My thousand dollars in front money was but a memory and the remaining four big ones were never to be mine, and at one o'clock my nameless friend would be sipping his Scotch and wondering why I'd decided to stand him up.

Oh, sure he would.

Chapter Five

I DON'T know just when I got to sleep. A little after midnight a wave of exhaustion hit me and I got out of my clothes and into Rod's bed. I was just on the verge of sleep when I sensed an alien presence hovering at the bedside. I told myself I was being silly, and you know how well that sort of thing works, and I opened my eyes and saw that the alien presence was a split-leaf philodendron on a small stand by the side of the bed. It had as much right to be there as I did, if not more, but by the time we'd taken each other's measure I was awake again, my mind spinning around in frenzied circles and not getting anywhere.

I switched on the radio part of Rod's stereo, set the volume low, and perched in a chair waiting for the music to end and the news to come on. You know how when you want music there's a newscast every fifteen minutes? Well, the reverse is just as true. Cops, taxis, newscasts, nothing's ever there when you want it.

Ultimately there *was* a newscast, of course, and I listened intently to any number of items in which I had no interest whatsoever, and the round-voiced announcer did not have Word One to say about a burglary and murder on East Sixty-seventh Street. Nada. Zip.

I switched to another station but of course I had half an hour to wait for their newscast, having just missed it, and they were playing a bland sort of folk-rock. When the singer started telling me that his girl's voice was a stick of chalk drawn across the blackboard of his soul (I swear I'm not making this up) I remembered I was hungry. I went to the kitchen and opened drawers and cabinets and peered inside the fridge, and you'd have thought Old Mother Hubbard lived there. I managed to turn up half a box of Uncle Ben's Converted Rice (formerly Buddhist and now Presbyterian, I suppose), a discouraging-looking can of Norwegian sardines in mustard sauce, and a lot of little jars and tins of herbs and spices and sauces which could have perked up food if there had been any around. I decided I'd make myself some rice, but a look into the box showed me that I was not the first uninvited guest to take note of it, and Uncle Ben had been further converted, this time from rice to roach shit.

In another cupboard I found an unopened box of spaghetti, which I decided might be palatable with olive oil provided that the oil wasn't rancid, which it was. At this stage I began to think that perhaps I wasn't hungry after all, and then I opened another cupboard and discovered that Rodney Hart was a soup fiend. There were sixty-three cans of Campbell's soup in that cupboard, and I know the exact number because I counted them, and I counted them because I wanted to know just how long I could stay alive without leaving the apartment. At the concentration-camp rate of a can a day I was good for two months, and that was plenty of time, I told myself, because long before my soup ran out the police would arrest me and in no time at all I'd be serving a sentence for first-degree murder, and feeding me would be the state's problem.

So there was really nothing to worry about after all.

I started to shake a little but forced myself to concentrate on the process of opening the can. Rod's can opener was pretty primitive, considering that soup was the mainstay of his existence, but it did the job. I dumped concentrated Chicken With Stars soup into a presumably clean saucepan, added water, heated the mess on the stove, pepped it up with a little thyme and a dash of soy sauce, and was sitting down to eat it just as the folk-rock station came through with a five-minute news summary. It repeated some of the items I'd already heard on the jazz station, told me far more than I needed to know about the weather, since I didn't dare go out in it anyway, and had nothing to say about the late J. F. Flaxford or the murderous burglar who had done him in.

I finished my soup and tidied up in the kitchen. Then I went through some more cupboards until I found Rod's booze collection, which consisted in the main of things like a bottle of ancient blackberry brandy with perhaps an ounce of the crud left in the bottom of it. That sort of treasure. But there was, incredibly, a fifth of Scotch about two-thirds full. Now this particular Scotch was some liquor store's private label, and it had been bottled over in Hackensack, so what we had here was not quite in the Chivas and Pinch class.

But burglars can't be choosers. I sat up for what was probably a long time, sipping Scotch and watching the really late movies on Channel 9, switching every half hour (when I remembered) to check out the radio news. Nothing about J. Francis, nothing about me, though after a while I probably could have heard the item and not paid any attention to it.

In one of those drab hours just before dawn I managed to kill the television set (having already done as much for the bottle) and insert myself a second time between Rodney's sheets.

The very next thing I knew there was a crashing noise and a girl's voice saying, "Oh, *shit!*"

No ONE ever returned more abruptly to consciousness. I had been deep in dreamless sleep and now I was jarringly awake. And there was someone in the apartment with me, someone female, and judging by her voice she was in rather close proximity to my no-longer-sleeping form.

I lay very still, trying to go on breathing as one breathes in sleep, hoping that she had not noticed my presence even as I realized that this was impossible. Who was she, anyway? And what the hell was she doing here?

And how was I going to get out of this mess?

"Shit," she said again, taking the word right out of my mouth. This time the syllable was addressed not to the Fates but to me. "I woke you up, didn't I? I was trying not to. I was being so quiet, just slipping around watering the plants, and then I had to go and knock the stupid thing over. I hope I didn't hurt the plant. And I'm sorry I disturbed you."

"It's all right," I told my pillow, keeping my face to it.

"I guess my plant-watering talents won't be needed anymore," she went on. "Will you be staying here for a while?"

"A couple of weeks."

"Rod didn't mention anything about anyone staying here. I guess you just got in recently, huh?"

Damn her, anyway. "Late last night," I said.

"Well, I'm terribly sorry I woke you up. I'll tell you what I'll do. I'll make us a cup of coffee."

"There's just soup."

"Soup?"

I rolled reluctantly over and blinked at her. She was at the side of the bed. She had the split-leaf philodendron back on its perch and she was pouring water at its roots. The plant didn't look any the worse for wear and she looked terrific.

Hair short and dark, a high forehead, and very precisely measured facial features with just the slightest upward tilt to her nose and just the right amount of determination in her jawline. A well-formed mouth that, if not generous, was by no means parsimonious. Little pink ears with well-defined lobes. (I'd recently read a paperback on determining character and health from ears, so I was noticing such things. Her ears, according to my source, would seem to be ideal.)

She was wearing white painter's pants which showed good judgment by hugging her tightly. They were starting to go thin at the knees and in the seat. Her shirt was denim, one of those Western-style numbers with pearlish buttons and floral print trim. She had a red bandanna around her neck and deerskin moccasins upon her little feet.

The only thing I could think of that was wrong with her was that she was there in my apartment. (Well, Rod's apartment.) She was watering his plants and jeopardizing my security. Yet when I thought of all the mornings I had awakened alone and would have been delighted to have had this very person in the room with me—ah, the injustice of it all. Women, policemen, taxis, newscasts, none of them on hand when you want them.

"Soup?" She turned her face toward me and smiled a tentative smile. Her eyes were either blue or green or both. Her teeth were white and even. "What kind of soup?"

"Almost any kind you'd want. Black bean soup, chicken noodle soup, cream of asparagus soup, tomato soup, cheddar cheese soup—"

"You're kidding about the cheddar cheese soup."

"Have I ever lied to you? It's in the cupboard if you don't believe me. If Campbell's makes it, Rod stocks it. And nothing else except for some roach-ridden rice."

"I guess he's not terribly domestic. Have you known him long?"

"We're old friends." A lie. "But I haven't seen very much of him in the past few years." A veritable truth.

"College friends? Or back in Illinois?"

Damn. What college? Where in Illinois? "College," I ventured.

"And now you've come to New York and you're staying at his place until—" the blue or green eyes widened "—until what? You're not an actor, are you?"

I agreed that I wasn't. But what in hell was I? I improvised a quick story, sitting up in bed with the sheet covering me to the throat. I told her how I'd been in the family feed business back home in South Dakota, that we'd been bought out at a good price by a competitor, and that I wanted to spend some time on my own in New York before I decided what turn my life should take next. I made the story very sincere and very dull, hoping she'd lose interest and remember a pressing engagement, but apparently she found my words more fascinating than I did because she hung on every one of them, sitting on the edge of my bed with her fingers interlaced around her knees and her eyes wide and innocent.

"You want to find yourself," she said. "That's very interesting."

"Well, I never even suspected that I was lost. But now that I'm really at loose ends—"

"I'm in the same position myself, in a way. I was divorced four years ago. Then I was working, not a very involving job, and then I quit, and now I'm on unemployment. I paint a little and I make jewelry and there's a thing I've been doing lately with stained glass. Not what everybody else does but a form I sort of invented myself, these three-dimensional free-form sculptures I've been making. The thing is, I don't know about any of these things, whether I'm good enough or not. I mean, maybe they're just hobbies. And if that's all they are, well, the hell with them. Because I don't want hobbies. I want something to do and I don't have it yet. Or at least I don't think I do." Her eyelashes fluttered at me. "You don't really want soup for breakfast, do you? Because why don't I run around the corner for coffee, it won't take me a minute, and you can put on some clothes and I'll be right back."

She was on her way out the door before I had any chance to object. When it closed behind her I got out of bed and went to the toilet. (I would avoid mentioning this, but it was the first time in a long time that I knew what I was doing.) Then I put on yesterday's clothes and sat in my favorite chair and waited to see what came through my door next.

Because it might well be the plant-watering lady with the coffee come to serve breakfast to the earnest young man from South Dakota.

Or it might be the minions of the law.

"I'll just run around the corner for coffee." Sure. Meaning she'd just recognized the notorious murdering burglar, or burgling murderer (or bungling mumbler, or what you will), and was

taking this opportunity to (a) escape his clutches and (b) let Justice be done.

I thought about running but couldn't see any real sense in it. As long as there was a chance she wasn't going to the cops, then this apartment was a damn sight safer than the streets. At least that's how my reasoning went, but I suspect the main factor was inertia. I had a bloodstream full of last night's lousy Scotch and a head full of rusty hardware and it was easier to sit than to run.

I could drag this out, but why? I didn't have to wait for the door to open to know she'd come back alone. I heard her steps on the stairs, and there is just no way that a herd of cops can ascend a staircase and sound in the process like a diminutive young lady. So I was relaxed and at ease long before the door opened, but when it did in fact open and her pert and pretty face appeared, I must confess it pleased me. Lots.

She had bought real coffee, astonishingly enough, and she now proceeded to make a pot of it. While she did this we chatted idly and easily. I'd had a chance to practice my lies during her absence, so when she told me her name was Ruth Hightower I was quick to reply that I was Roger Armitage. From that point on we ruthed and rogered one another relentlessly.

I said something about the airlines having lost my luggage, tossing the line in before it could occur to her to wonder at my lack of possessions. She said the airlines were always doing that and we both agreed that a civilization that could put a man on the moon ought to be able to keep track of a couple of suitcases. We pulled up chairs on either side of a table and we drank our coffee out of Rod's chipped and unmatched cups. It was good coffee.

We talked and talked and talked, and I fell into the role so completely that I became quite comfortable in it. Perhaps it was the influence of the environment, perhaps the apartment was making an actor out of me. Rod had said the landlord liked actors. Perhaps the whole building swarmed with them, perhaps it was something in the walls and woodwork. . . .

At any rate I was a perfect Roger Armitage, the new boy in town, and she was the lady I'd met under cute if clumsy circumstances, and before too long I found myself trying to figure out an offhand way to ask her just how well she knew Rod, and just what sort of part he played in her life, and, uh, shucks Ma'am—

But what the hell did it matter? Whatever future our relationship had was largely in the past. As soon as she left I'd have to think about clearing out myself. This was not a stupid lady, and sooner or later she would figure out just who I was, and when that happened it would behoove me to be somewhere else.

And then she was saying, "You know, I was trying so hard to take care of those plants and get out before I woke you, and actually what I should have done was just leave right away because you would have taken care of the plants yourself, but I didn't think of that, and you know something? I'm glad I didn't. I'm really enjoying this conversation."

"So am I, Ruth."

"You're easy to talk to. Usually I have trouble talking to people. Especially to men."

"It's hard to believe you're not at ease with everyone."

"What a nice thing to say!" Her eyes—I'd learned by now that they ranged from blue to green, varying either with her mood or with the way the light hit them—her eyes, as I was saying way back at the beginning of this sentence, gazed shyly up at me from beneath lowered lashes. "It's turned into a nice day, hasn't it?"

"Yes, it has."

"It's a little chilly out but the sky is clear. I thought about picking up some sweet rolls but I didn't know whether you'd want anything besides just coffee."

"Just coffee is fine. And this is good coffee."

"Another cup? Here, I'll get it for you."

"Thanks."

"What should I call you, Bernie or Bernard?"

"Whichever you like."

"I think I'll call you Bernie."

"Most people do," I said. "Oh, sweet suffering Jesus," I said.

"It's all right, Bernie."

"God in Heaven."

"It's all right." She leaned across the table toward me, a smile flickering at the corners of her mouth, and she placed a small soft-palmed hand atop mine. "There's nothing to worry about," she said.

"There isn't?"

"Of course not. I know you didn't kill anybody. I'm an extremely intuitive person. If I hadn't been pretty sure you were innocent I wouldn't have gone to the trouble of knocking the plant over in the first place, and—"

"You knocked it over on purpose?"

"Uh-huh. The stand, anyway. I picked up the plant itself so nothing would happen to it, and then I kicked the stand so that it bounced off the wall and fell over."

"Then you knew all along."

"Well, your name's all over the papers, Bernie. And it's also all over your driver's license and the other papers in your wallet. I went through your pockets while you were sleeping. You're one of the soundest sleepers I've come across."

"Do you come across that many?"

Incredibly enough, the minx blushed. "Not all that many, no. Where was I?"

"Going through my pockets."

"Yes. I thought I recognized you. There was a photo in the *Times* this morning. It's not a very good likeness. Do they really cut a person's hair that short when they send him to prison?"

"Ever since Samson pushed the temple down. They're not taking any chances."

"I think it's barbaric of them. Anyway, the minute I looked at you I knew you couldn't have murdered that Flaxford person. You're not a murderer." She frowned a little. "But I guess you're a genuine burglar, aren't you?"

"It does look that way."

"It certainly does, doesn't it? Do you really know Rod?"

"Not terribly well. We've played poker together a few times."

"But he doesn't know what you do for a living, does he? And how come he gave you his keys? Oh, I'm being dull-witted now. What would you need with keys? I saw your keys in your pants pocket, and all those other implements. I must say they look terribly efficient. Don't you need something called a jimmy to pry doors open with?"

"Only if you're crude."

"But you're not, are you? There's something very sexual about burglary, isn't there? How on earth did you get into a business like that? But the man's supposed to ask the girl that question, isn't he? My, we have a lot to talk about, and it should be a lot more interesting than all that crap about Roger Armitage and the feed business in South Dakota, and I'll bet you've never even been to South Dakota, have you? Although you do string out a fairly convincing pack of lies. Would you like some more coffee, Bernie?"

"Yes," I said. "Yes, I think I would."

Chapter Six

By six twenty-four that evening the chaps at Channel 7 had said all they were likely to say about the five-state manhunt now under way for Bernard Rhodenbarr, gentleman burglar turned blood-crazed killer. I set one of the foxy old Colonel's better chicken legs on my plate and crossed the room to turn off Rod's Panasonic. Ruth sat cross-legged on the floor, a chicken leg of her own unattended while she muttered furiously about the perfidy of Ray Kirschmann. "The gall of that man," she said. "Taking a thousand dollars of your hard-earned money and then saying such horrible things about you."

In Ray's version of the proceedings, I'd crouched in the shadows to take him and Loren by surprise; only his daring and perseverance had enabled him to identify me during the fracas. "I've felt for years that Rhodenbarr was capable of violence," he'd told the reporters, and it seemed to me that his baleful glower had been directed not at the TV cameras but through them at me.

"Well, I let him down," I said. "Made him look foolish in front of his partner."

"Do you think he really believed what he said?"

"That I killed Flaxford? Of course he does. You and I are the only people in the world who think otherwise."

"And the real killer."

"And the real killer," I agreed. "But he's not likely to speak up and nobody's going to take my word for anything, and you can't do much in the way of proving your case. As a matter of fact, I don't see why you believe me to begin with."

"You have an honest face."

"For a burglar, maybe."

"And I'm a very intuitive person."

"So I've been given to understand."

"J. Francis Flaxford," she said.

"May he rest in peace."

"Amen. You know, I can never bring myself to trust men who turn their first name into an initial that way. I always feel they're leading some sort of secret life. There's just something devious about the way they perceive themselves and the image they present to the world."

"That's quite a generalization, isn't it?"

"Oh, I don't know. Look at the record. G. Gordon Liddy, E. Howard Hunt—"

"Fellow burglars, both of them."

"Do you have a middle name, Bernie?"

I nodded. "Grimes," I said. "My mother's maiden name."

"Would you ever call yourself B. Grimes Rhodenbarr?"

"I never have. Somehow I doubt I ever shall. But if I did it wouldn't mean I was trying to hide something. It would mean I had taken leave of my senses. B. Grimes Rhodenbarr, for God's sake! Look, plenty of people have first names they're not nuts about, and they like their middle names, so—"

"Then they can drop their first names entirely," she said. "That's open and aboveboard enough. It's when they keep that sneaky little initial out in front there that I don't trust them." She showed me the tip of her tongue. "Anyway, I like my theory. And I wouldn't dream of trusting J. Francis Flaxford."

"I think you can trust him now. Being dead means never having to do anything sneaky."

"I wish we knew more about him. All we really know is that he's dead."

"Well, it's the most salient fact about him. If he weren't dead we wouldn't have to know anything at all about the sonofabitch."

"You shouldn't call him that, Bernie."

"I suppose not."

"*De mortuis* and all that."

De mortuis indeed. She gnawed the last of the meat from her chicken bone, then gathered together all of our leavings and carried them to the kitchen. I watched her little bottom as she walked, and when she bent over to deposit the chicken bones in the garbage I got a lump in my throat, among other things. Then she straightened up and set about pouring two cups of coffee and I made myself think about the late Francis Flaxford, with a J. in front of his name and an R.I.P. after it.

The night before I'd wondered idly if the dead man was actually Flaxford. Maybe some other burglar had been working the same side of the street, taking advantage of Flaxford's scheduled absence and arriving there before me. Then he'd managed to get his head dented and had been there when I showed up.

But who would have killed him? Flaxford himself?

No matter. The corpse was truly Flaxford, a forty-eight-year-old entrepreneur and dabbler in real estate, a producer of off-off-Broadway theatrical ventures, a *bon vivant*, a man about town. He'd been married and divorced years and years ago, he'd lived alone in his plush East Side apartment, and someone had smashed his skull with an ashtray.

"If you were going to kill somebody," Ruth said, "you wouldn't use an ashtray, would you?"

"He liked substantial ashtrays," I told her. "There was one in the living room that would have felled an ox. A big cut-glass thing, and they say the murder weapon was a cut-glass ashtray, and if it was a mate to the one I saw it would have done the job, all right." I looked at the *Post* story again, tapped a fingernail against his picture. "He wasn't bad-looking," I said.

"If you like the type."

He had a good-looking, high-browed face, a mane of dark hair going gray at the temples, a moustache that his barber had taken pains to trim.

"Distinguished," I said.

"If you say so."

"Even elegant."

"Try sneaky and shifty while you're at it."

"*De mortuis*, remember?"

"Oh, screw *de mortuis*. As my grandmother used to say, if you've got nothing good to say about someone, let's hear it. I wonder how he really made his money, Bernie. What do you suppose he did for a living?"

"He was an entrepreneur, it says here."

"That just means he made money. It doesn't explain how."

"He dabbled in real estate."

"That's something you do with money, like producing plays off-off-Broadway. The real estate may have made money for him and the plays must have lost it, they always do, but he must have done something for a living and I'll bet it was faintly crooked."

"You're probably right."

"So why isn't it in the paper?"

"Because nobody cares. As far as everybody's concerned, he only got killed because he was in the wrong place at the wrong time. A mad-dog burglar happened to pick his apartment at random and he happened to be in it, and that was when J. Francis kept his appointment in Samarra. If he'd been wearing ladies' underwear at the time of his death he'd make better copy and the reporters would take a longer look at his life, but instead he was just wearing a perfectly ordinary Brooks Brothers dressing gown and that made him dull copy."

"Where does it say he was wearing a Brooks Brothers robe?"

"I made that up. I don't know where he bought his clothes. It just says he was wearing a dressing gown. The *Times* says dressing gown. The *Post* calls it a bathrobe."

"I had the impression he was naked."

"Not according to the working press." I tried to remember if Loren had blurted out anything about his dress or lack of it. If he did, I didn't remember it. "He'll probably be naked in tomorrow morning's *Daily News*," I said. "What difference does it make?"

"It doesn't."

We were sitting side by side on the Lawson couch. She folded the paper and put it on the seat beside her. "I just wish we had someplace to start," she said. "But it's like trying to untie a knot when both ends of the rope are out of sight. All we've got are the dead man and the man who got you mixed up in this in the first place."

"And we don't know who he is."

"Mr. Shmoo. Mr. Chocolate Eyes. A man with narrow shoulders and a large waistline who avoids looking people right in the eye."

"That's our man."

"And he looks vaguely familiar to you."

"He looks specifically familiar to me. He even sounded familiar."

"But you never met him before."

"Never."

"Damn." She made fists of her hands, pressed them against her thighs. "Could you have known him in prison?"

"I don't think so. That would be logical, wouldn't it? Then of course he would have known I was a burglar. But I can't think of any area of my life in or out of prison that he fits into. Maybe I've seen him on subways, passed him in the street. That sort of thing."

"Maybe." She frowned. "He set you up. Either he killed Flaxford himself or he knows who did."

"I don't think he killed anybody."

"But he must know who did."

"Probably."

"So if we could just find him. I know you don't know his name, but did he give you a fake name at least?"

"No. Why?"

"We could try paging him at that bar. I forget the name."

"Pandora's. Why page him?"

"I don't know. Maybe you could tell him you had the blue leather box."

"*What* blue leather box?"

"The one you went to—oh."

"There isn't any blue leather box."

"Of course not," she said. "There never was one in the first place, was there? The blue leather box was nothing but a red herring." She wrinkled up her forehead in concentration. "But then why did he arrange to meet you at Pandora's?"

"I don't know. I'm sure he didn't bother to show up."

"Then why arrange it?"

"Beats me. Unless he planned to tip the police if I showed up there, but I don't think that makes any sense either. Maybe he just wanted to go through the motions of setting up a meeting. To make the whole thing seem authentic." I closed my eyes for a moment, running the scene through my mind. "I'll tell you what's funny. I have the feeling he kept trying to impress me with how tough he was. Why would he do that?"

"So you'd be afraid to double-cross him, I suppose."

"But why would I cross him in the first place? There's something funny about the guy. I think he was pretending to be tough because he's not. Not tough, I mean. He talked the talk but he didn't walk the walk. I suppose he must have been a con artist of some sort." I grinned. "He certainly conned me. It's hard to believe there was no blue box in that apartment. He had me convinced that it was there and that he really didn't want me to open it."

"You don't remember him from jail. Do you think he's ever been arrested?"

"Probably. It sort of comes with the territory. However good you are, sooner or later you step in the wrong place. I told you about my last arrest, didn't I?"

"When the bell was out of order."

"Right, and I wound up tossing an apartment while the tenants were home. And I had to pick a man with a gun and an air of righteous indignation, and then when I told him how we ought to be able to be reasonable about this and pulled out my walking money, he turned out to be the head of some civic group. I'd have had about as much chance of bribing a rabbi with a ham sandwich. They didn't just throw the book at me, they threw the whole library."

"Poor Bernie," she said, and put her hand on mine. Our hands took a few minutes to get acquainted. Our eyes met, then slipped away to leave us with our private thoughts.

And mine turned, not for the first time, to prison. If I gave myself up they'd undoubtedly let me cop a plea to Murder Two, maybe even some degree of manslaughter. I'd most likely be on the street in three or four years with good time and parole and all that. I'd never served that much time before, but my last stretch had been substantial enough, eighteen months, and if you can do eighteen months you can do four years. Either way you straighten up and square your shoulders and do your bit one day at a time.

Of course I was older now and I'd be crowding forty by the time I got out. But they say it's easier to do time when you're older because the months and the years seem to pass more rapidly.

No women inside. No soft cool hands, no taut rounded bottoms. (There are men inside with taut rounded bottoms, if you happen to like that sort of thing. I don't happen to like that sort of thing.)

"Bernie? I could go to the police."

"And turn me in? It might make sense if there was a reward, but—"

"What are you talking about? Why would I turn you in? Are you crazy?"

"A little. Why else would you go to the cops?"

"Don't they have books full of pictures of criminals? I could tell them I was taken by a con man and get them to show me pictures."

"And then what?"

"Well, maybe I'd recognize him."

"You've never seen him, Ruth."

"I feel as though I have from your description."

"A mug shot would just show his face. Not his profile."

"Oh."

"That's why they call it a mug shot."

"Oh."

"I don't think it's a viable approach."

"I guess not, Bernie."

I turned her hand over, stroked the palm and the pads of her fingers. She moved her body a little closer to mine. We sat like that for a few minutes while I got myself all prepared to put my arm around her, and just as I was about to make my move she stood up.

"I just wish we could *do* something," she said. "If we knew the name of the man who roped you in we would at least have a place to start."

"Or if we knew why somebody wanted to kill Flaxford. Somebody had a reason to want him dead. A motive. If we knew more about him we might know what to look for."

"Don't the police—"

"The police already know who killed him. There won't ever be any investigation, Ruth, because as far as they're concerned I'm guilty and the case is closed. All they have to do is get their hands on me. That's why the frame works so perfectly. It may be that there's only one person in the world with a motive for killing Flaxford, but no one will ever know about it because Flaxford's murder is all wrapped up and tied with a ribbon and the card has my name on it."

"I could go to the library tomorrow. I'll check *The New York Times Index.* Maybe they ran something on him years ago and I can read all about it in the microfilm room."

I shook my head. "If there was anything juicy they'd have dug it up and run it in his obit."

"There might be something that would make some kind of connection for us. It's worth a try, isn't it?"

"I suppose so."

She walked half a dozen steps in one direction, then retraced them, then turned and began the process anew. It was a reasonably good Caged Lion impression. "I can't just sit around," she said. "I get stir crazy."

"You'd hate prison."

"God! How do people stand it?"

"A day at a time," I said. "I'd take you out for a night on the town, Ruth, but—"

"No, you have to stay here," she said. "I realize that." She picked up one of the papers, turned pages. "Maybe there's something on television," she said, and it turned out that there was a Warner Brothers gangster thing on WPIX. The whole crew was in it—Robinson, Lorre, Greenstreet, and a ton of great old character actors whose names I've never bothered to learn but whose faces I'd never forget. She sat on the couch next to me and we watched the whole thing, and eventually I did manage to put an arm around her and we sort of cuddled, doing a little low-level necking during the commercials.

When the last villain got his and they rolled the final credits she said, "See? The bad guys always lose in the end. We've got nothing to worry about."

"Life," I announced, "is not a B picture."

"Well, it ain't no De Mille epic either, boss. Things'll work out, Bernie."

"Maybe."

The eleven o'clock news came on and we watched it until they got to the part we were interested in. There were no new developments in the Flaxford murder, and the report they gave was just an abbreviated version of what we'd seen a few hours earlier. When they cut to an item about a drug bust in Hunts Point Ruth went over to the set and turned it off.

"I guess I'll go now," she said.

"Go?"

"Home."

"Where's that?"

"Bank Street. Not far from here."

"You could stick around," I suggested. "There's probably something watchable on the tube."

"I'm pretty tired, actually. I was up early this morning."

"Well, you could, uh, sleep here," I said. "As far as that goes."

"I don't think so, Bernie."

"I hate to think of you walking home alone. At this hour and in this neighborhood—"

"It's not even midnight yet. And this is the safest neighborhood in the city."

"It's sort of nice having you around," I said.

She smiled. "I really want to go home tonight," she said. "I want to shower and get out of these clothes—"

"So?"

"—and I have to feed my cats. The poor little things must be starving."

"Can't they open a can?"

"No, they're hopelessly spoiled. Their names are Esther and Mordecai. They're Abyssinians."

"Then why did you give them Hebrew names?"

"What else would I call them, Haile and Selassie?"

"That's a point."

I followed her to the door. She turned with one hand on the knob and we kissed, and it was very nice. I really wanted her to stay, and she made a rather encouraging sound down deep in her throat and ground herself against me a little.

Then I let go of her and she opened the door and said, "See you tomorrow, Bernie."

And left.

Chapter Seven

THE subway wasn't doing much business by the time I got onto it. I caught an uptown Eighth Avenue local at Fourteenth Street and there was only one other person in the car with me. That was the good news. The bad news is that he was a Transit Authority cop with an enormous revolver on his hip. He kept looking at me because there was nobody else for him to look at, and I just knew that he was going to figure out why I looked familiar. At any moment a lightbulb would form in the air over his head and he would spring into action.

Except he never did. At Times Square we picked up some fellow travelers—a pair of off-duty nurses, an utterly wasted junkie—and that gave the cop someplace else to focus his eyes. Then at Fifty-ninth Street he got off, and a stop later it was my turn. I climbed the stairs and emerged into the early morning air at Seventy-second and Central Park West and wondered what the hell I thought I was doing.

Earlier that evening I'd been completely comfortable sitting around Rod's apartment with my eyes on the television set and my arm around Ruth. But once she was gone I began finding the place unbearable. I couldn't sit still, couldn't watch the tube, kept pacing around and getting increasingly twitchy. A little after midnight I took a shower, and when the prospect of putting on the same clothes seemed as appalling as you might imagine it would, I went through Rod's closet and dresser to see what he'd left behind.

There wasn't much I could use. Either he tended to take an awful lot of clothing on the road with him or he didn't own much in the first place. I found a shirt I could wear, although I didn't much want to, and a pair of navy blue stretch socks, but that was about the extent of it.

Then I came across the wig.

It was a blondish wig, long but not quite hippie in style. I put it on and checked myself out in the mirror and I was astonished at the transformation. The only problem was that it was a little too garish and drew a little too much attention, but that problem was solved when I found a cloth cap on a shelf in the closet. The cap softened the effect of the wig and made it less of an attention-getter.

Anyone who knew me personally would recognize me, I decided. But a stranger passing me on the street would just see yellow hair and a cloth cap.

I told myself I was crazy. I took off the cap and the wig and sat down in front of the television set. After a few minutes the phone started to ring, and it went on ringing twenty-two times by actual count before the caller gave up or the service did what it was supposed to do. The phone had rung periodically during the day— Ruth almost answered it once—but it had never gone so long unattended.

At a quarter to one I put on the wig and the cap and got out of there.

FROM the subway I walked over to my apartment building. I'd taken the subway instead of a cab because I hadn't wanted to talk to anyone on a one-to-one basis. Maybe on some level or other I was worried that I'd run into the cabbie who'd driven me around the night before. But once I had to walk those few blocks to my building I began wishing I'd done things the other way around. There were a lot of people on Seventy-second Street and it was brightly lit, and I'd lived in that neighborhood for several years. In the course of a short walk I saw several people whom I recognized. I didn't know their names but I'd seen them on the streets at one time or another, and it was logical to assume they'd seen me and could recognize me if they took a good long look at me. I tried to assume a posture and a rhythm of walking that was not my usual style. Maybe it helped. In any event, nobody seemed to notice me.

Finally I was standing in the shadows on the corner diagonally across the street from where I lived. I gazed up and found my window up there on the sixteenth floor facing south. My apartment. My little chunk of private space.

God knows it wasn't much, two small rooms and a kitchen, an overpriced cubicle in a sterile modern building. The view was the only charm the place had. But it was home, dammit, and I'd been comfortable here.

All that was over now. Even if I got out of this mess (and I couldn't really imagine how that could happen) I didn't see how I could go on living here. Because now they all knew the horrible truth about that pleasant chap in 16-G. He was a burglar, for God's sake. A criminal.

I thought of all the people I nodded to daily in the elevator, the women I'd exchanged pleasantries with in the laundry room, the doormen and hall porters, the super and the handyman. Mrs. Hesch, the chain-smoking old lady across the hall from whom I could always borrow a cup of detergent. She was the only person there that I really knew, and I don't suppose I knew her very well, but I was on amicable terms with all those people and I'd liked living among them.

Now I couldn't go back there. Bernard Rhodenbarr, burglar. I'd have to move somewhere else, have to use some sort of alias to rent an apartment. Jesus, it's hard enough functioning as a professional criminal, but when you have the added burden of notoriety you're really up against it.

Could I possibly risk going upstairs? The midnight-to-eight doorman, a stout old fellow named Fritz, was on his post. I didn't really think the cap and the wig would fool him. It was possible that a couple of bucks would blind him to his civic duty, but it was also possible that it would not, and the downside risk seemed dis-proportionate to the possible gain. On the other hand, there was a side entrance, a flight of stairs leading to the basement. They kept that entrance locked; you could get out through it from inside, and the super would unlock it for deliveries, but you couldn't get in.

You couldn't get in. *I* could.

From the basement I could catch the self-service elevator straight upstairs, past the lobby to the sixteenth floor. And I could let myself out the same way, and I could carry with me a suitcase full of clothes and my five thousand dollars in case money. If I did turn myself in, or if they grabbed me, I had to have money for a lawyer. And I wanted to have the money on me, not tucked away in an apartment that I wouldn't be allowed to go to.

I fingered my ring of keys and picks, stepped out of the shadows and started to cross Seventy-first Street. Just as I reached the opposite corner a car pulled up in front of my building and parked at a hydrant. It was an ordinary late-model sedan but there was something about the nonchalance with which the driver dumped it next to the hydrant that shouted *cop* to me.

Two men got out of the car. I didn't recognize them and there was nothing obviously coppish about their appearance. They were wearing suits and ties, but lots of people do that, not just plainclothes detectives.

I stayed on my side of West End Avenue. And sure enough they showed something to Fritz, and I stayed where I was, backing away from the curb, as a matter of fact, and placing myself alongside the stoop of a brownstone where I wouldn't be noticeable. Anyone who noticed me would take me for a mugger and give me a wide berth.

I just stood there for a minute. Then it occurred to me that I'd like to have a look at my window, so I crossed back to the corner I'd occupied originally and counted up to the sixteenth floor and over to the G apartment, and the light was on.

I stayed there for fifteen long minutes and the light went right on blazing away. I scratched my head, a dumb thing to do when you're wearing a loose-fitting wig. I rearranged the wig and the cap and wondered what the bastards were doing in my apartment and just how long it would take them to do it.

Too long, I decided. And they'd be noisy, there being no reason for them to toss my place in silence, so that if I went in after them my neighbors might very well be sensitive to sounds, and . . .

The hell with it.

I WALKED FOR A WHILE. I KEPT to residential streets and stayed away from streetlights, walking around and trying to figure out what to do next. Eventually I found myself just half a block from Pandora's. I found a spot where I could watch the doorway without being terribly noticeable myself and I stood there until I got a cramp in my calf and became very much aware of a dryness in my throat. I don't know just how long I stood there but it was long enough for eight or ten people to enter the saloon and about as many to leave. None of them was my little pear-shaped friend.

Maybe I'd seen him around the neighborhood. Maybe that was why he looked familiar to me. Maybe I used to pass him regularly on the streets and his face and figure had registered on some subliminal level. Maybe he'd mentioned Pandora's because it was his regular hangout and the first place that came to mind, even though he'd had no intention whatsoever of keeping our appointment.

Maybe he was inside there right now.

I don't honestly think I believed this for a minute. But I was thirsty enough to grab at a straw if it meant I could grab at a beer. The faint possibility of his presence in the place enabled me to rationalize going inside myself.

And of course he wasn't there, but the beer was good.

I DIDN'T stay there long, and when I left I had a bad couple of minutes. I was convinced someone was following me. I was heading south on Broadway and there was a man twenty or thirty yards back of me who I was sure had come out of the bar after me. I turned right at Sixtieth Street and so did he, and this didn't do wonders for my morale.

I crossed the street and went on walking west. He stayed on his side of the street. He was a smallish chap and he wore a poplin windbreaker over dark slacks and a light shirt. I couldn't see much of his face in that light and I didn't want to stop and stare at him anyway.

Just before I reached Columbus Avenue he crossed over to my side of the street. I turned downtown on Columbus, which becomes Ninth Avenue at about that point, and to the surprise of practically no one he turned the corner and followed me. I tried to figure out what to do. I could try to shake him, I could pop into a doorway and deck him when he came by, or I could just keep walking and see what he did.

I kept walking, and a block farther on he ducked into a saloon and that was the end of him. He was just another poor bastard looking for a drink.

I walked to Columbus Circle and took a subway home. Well, to my home away from home, anyway. This time I had less difficulty finding Bethune Street. It was right where I left it. I opened the downstairs door about as quickly as I could have managed if I had a key to it, scampered up the four miserable flights of stairs, and was in Rod's apartment in no time at all. I had no trouble with the three locks because I hadn't had a key to lock them with when I left. Only the spring lock was engaged, and I loided it with a strip of flexible steel, an operation that honestly takes less time than opening it with a key.

Then I fastened all the locks and went to bed. I hadn't accomplished a thing and I'd taken any number of brainless chances, but all the same I lay there in Rod's bed and felt pleased with myself. I'd gone out on the street instead of hiding, I'd gone through the motions of taking some responsibility for myself.

It felt good.

Chapter Eight

SHE didn't have to knock any plants over the next morning. I was awake and out of bed a few minutes after nine. I took a shower and looked around for something to shave with. Rod had left his second-string razor behind. I found it in the medicine chest hiding behind an empty Band-Aid box. It was an obsolete Gillette that hadn't been used in at least a year and hadn't been cleaned in at least a year and a day. The old blade was still in it and so was the crud and whiskers from Rod's last shave with it. I held it under the faucet stream, but that was like trying to sweep out the Augean stables with a child's toy broom.

I decided to call Ruth and ask her to bring things like toothpaste and a toothbrush and shaving gear. I looked up Hightower in the Manhattan white pages and found it was a commoner name than I would have guessed, but none of the Hightowers were named Ruth or lived on Bank Street. I called Information and an operator with a Latin accent assured me that there were no listings in that name or on that street. After I'd put the phone down I told myself there was no reason to question the competence of a telephone operator just because English looked to be her second language, but all the same I dialed 411 again and put another operator through the same routine. Her accent was pure dulcet Flatbush and she didn't do any better at finding Ruth's number.

I decided she was probably unlisted. What the hell, she wasn't an actress. Why should she have a listed phone?

I turned on the television set for company, put up a pot of coffee, and went back and looked at the phone some more. I decided to dial my own number to see if there were any cops in the place at the moment. I picked up the phone, then put it down when I realized I wasn't sure of my number. It was one I never called, since when I was out there was never anybody home. This sort of surprised me; I mean, even if you never call your own number you have to know it to give it out to people. But I guess that doesn't happen often in my case. Anyway, I looked it up and there it was, and I'm happy to say I recognized it once I saw it. I dialed and nobody answered, which stood to reason, and I put the phone back in its cradle.

I was on my second cup of coffee when I heard footsteps ascending the staircase and approaching the door. She knocked but I let her use her keys. She came in, all bright-eyed and buoyant, carrying a small grocery bag and explaining that she'd brought bacon and eggs. "And you've already got coffee made," she said. "Great. Here's this morning's *Times*. There's not really anything in it."

"I didn't think there would be."

"I suppose I could have bought the *Daily News* too but I never do. I figure if anything really important happens the *Times* will tell me about it. Is this the only frying pan he owns?"

"Unless he took the others on tour with him."

"He's not very domestic at all. Well, we'll have to deal with the material at hand. I'm relatively new at harboring fugitives but I'll do my best to harbor you in the style to which you are accustomed. Is it called harboring a fugitive if you do it in somebody else's apartment?"

"It's called accessory after the fact to homicide," I said.

"That sounds serious."

"It ought to."

"Bernie—"

I took her arm. "I was thinking about that earlier, Ruth. Maybe you ought to bail out."

"Don't be ridiculous."

"You could wind up buying a lot of trouble."

"That's crazy," she said. "You're innocent, aren't you?"

"The cops don't think so."

"They will when we find the real killer for them. Hey, c'mon, Bern! I've seen all the old movies, remember? I know the good guys always come through in the end. We're the good guys, aren't we?"

"I'd certainly like to think so."

"Then we've got nothing to worry about. Now just tell me how you like your eggs and then get the hell out of here, huh? There's room for me and the roaches in this kitchen and that's about all. What are you doing, Bernie?"

"Kissing your neck."

"Oh. Well, that's okay, I guess. Actually you could do it some more if you'd like. Hmmmm. You know, that's sort of nice, Bernie. I could learn to like that."

We were polishing off the eggs when the phone rang. The service was on the ball and picked up midway through the fourth ring.

Which reminded me. "I tried to call you earlier," I said, "but your number's unlisted. Unless you've got it listed in your husband's name or something like that."

"Oh," she said. "No, it's unlisted. Why were you trying to call?"

"Because I need a shave."

"I noticed. Your face is all scratchy. Actually I sort of like it, but I can see where you'd want to shave."

I told her about the lack of shaving cream and the state of Rod's razor. "I thought you could pick them up on your way over here."

"I'll go get them now. It's no trouble."

"If I'd had your number I could have saved you a trip."

"Oh, it's no trouble," she said. "I don't mind. Is there anything else you need?"

I thought of a few things and she made a small list. I took a ten out of my wallet and made her take it. "There's really no rush," I said.

"I'd just as soon go now. I was just thinking, Bernie. Maybe it's not a good idea to use the telephone."

"Why not?"

"Well, couldn't the people at the service tell if it was off the hook or if you were talking to someone? I think they could even listen in, couldn't they?"

"Gee, I don't know. I've never understood just how those things work."

"And they know Rod's out of town, and if they knew someone was in his apartment—"

"Ruth, they usually let the phone ring twenty times before they get around to answering it. That's how efficient they are. The only time they pay attention to a subscriber's line is when it's ringing, and even then their attention isn't too terribly keen."

"The last time it rang they got it right away."

"Well, accidents happen, I suppose. But you don't really think there's any risk in using the phone, do you?"

"Well—"

"There can't be."

But when she went out I found myself standing next to the phone and staring at it as if it were a potential menace. I picked up the receiver and started dialing my own apartment—I remembered the number this time—but halfway through I decided the hell with it and hung up.

While she shopped I did up the breakfast dishes and read the paper. All the *Times* had to tell me was that I was still at large and I already knew that.

This time I hadn't bothered locking the door, and when she knocked I went over and opened it for her. She handed me a paper bag containing a razor, a small package of blades, shaving cream, a toothbrush and a small tube of toothpaste. She also gave me forty-seven cents change from my ten-dollar bill. Every once in a while something like that comes along to demonstrate that all this talk about inflation is not entirely unwarranted.

"I'll be going out in a few minutes," she said. "You can shave then."

"Out? You just got here."

"I know. I want to go to the library. And check the *Times Index*—we talked about that last night. I don't know how else we're going to learn anything about Flaxford unless I go track down his ex-wife and talk to her."

"That sounds like more trouble than it's likely to be worth."

"The *Times?* I just go to Forty-second and Fifth—"

"I know where the library is. I mean the ex-wife."

"Well, it might not be any trouble at all, actually. Do ex-wives come to memorial services for their ex-husbands? Because that's where I'm going this afternoon. There's a memorial service for him at two thirty. What's the difference between a memorial service and a funeral?"

"I don't know."

"I think it's whether or not you have the body around. I guess the police are probably hanging onto the body for an autopsy or something. To make sure he's really dead."

"They already established cause and time of death."

"Well, maybe they just aren't releasing the body, or maybe it's being shipped somewhere. *I* don't know. But that's the difference, isn't it? You can't have a funeral without a corpse, can you?"

"Tell that to Tom Sawyer."

"Funny. Maybe I'll go over to that bar. Pandora's Box."

"Just Pandora's. Why would you go there?"

"I don't know. The same reason I'm going to the memorial service, I suppose. On the chance that I might run into the little man who wasn't there."

"I don't see why he would be at the memorial service."

She shrugged. "I don't either. But if he's a business acquaintance of Flaxford's he might have to go, and anything's possible, isn't it? And if he's not at the service he might be drowning his sorrows at Pandora's."

And she went on to explain her reasons for thinking Pandora's might be our friend's regular hangout, and they were pretty much the same reasons which had led me to drop in there for a beer the night before. If he was at the bar or the memorial chapel, she felt certain she'd recognize him from my description.

We sat around talking about this and other things for perhaps another hour before she decided it was time for her to head uptown. Several times I was on the point of mentioning that I'd gone to Pandora's myself just a matter of hours ago, but for one reason or another I never did get around to it.

Once she was gone, the day sagged. She was out doing things, pointless or otherwise, and all I had to do was hang around and kill time. I decided I should have put on the wig and the cap and tagged along after her, and I decided that would have been pretty stupid, since the cops would certainly have a man on duty at the service just as a matter of routine. I found myself wondering if Ruth was aware of this possibility, and if she knew enough not to attract attention there or to be followed when she left.

When you have nothing better to worry about, you make do with what you've got. I decided I ought to let her know about this danger. But I couldn't call her because I didn't have her number and anyway she was going straight to the library. Of course I could call the library and have her paged, except I was by no means certain that they would page people, although I could always claim it was a matter of life and death. . . .

No, all that would do was draw attention. So I could put on the wig and the cap and go up to the library and tell her, and no doubt I would corner her in a room where three cops were browsing at the moment, and she'd call me by name, and my cap and wig would fall off.

So instead I went and shaved. I took as much time as possible doing this, soaping and rinsing my face four or five times first, then shaving very carefully and deliberately. I treated myself to the closest shave I'd had in years—unless you count my departure from the Flaxford apartment, heh heh—and I left my moustache unshaven, figuring that it might become a useful part of my disguise, no doubt combining nicely with wig and cap.

Then I dragged the cap and the yellow wig out of the closet and tried them on, and I scrutinized the patch of eighth-of-an-inch fur on my upper lip, and I returned wig and cap to closet shelf and lathered up again and erased the attempted moustache altogether.

And that was about the size of it. I had done as thorough a job of shaving as I possibly could, and the only way to invest more time in the process would be to shave my head. It's an indication of my state of mind that there was a point when I actually considered this, thinking that my wig would fit much better if I had no hair of my own underneath it. Fortunately the notion passed before I could do anything about it.

At one point I did dial my own apartment again, just out of boredom. I got a busy signal and it spooked me until I realized that it didn't necessarily mean my phone was off the hook. It could mean that the circuits were busy, which happens often enough, or it could mean that someone else was trying to call me and he'd gotten connected first. I tried a few minutes later and the phone rang and no one answered it.

I went back to the television set and hopped around the channels. WOR had some reruns of *Highway Patrol* and I sat back and watched Broderick Crawford giving somebody hell. He's always been great at that.

I took out my little ring of keys and picks and weighed it in my hand, while weighing in my head the possibility of giving some of the other apartments in the building a quick shuffle. Just to keep my hand in, say. I could check the buzzers downstairs, get the names, look them up in the phone book, determine over the phone who was home and who wasn't, and go door to door to see what would turn up. Some clothing in my size, say, or some cat food for Esther and Mordecai.

I never really gave this lunacy *serious* consideration. But I was so desperate for things to think about that I did give it some thought.

And then somewhere along the line I dozed off in front of the television set, paying token attention to the story until some indeterminate point where it faded out and my own equally uninspired dreams took over. I don't know exactly when I fell asleep so there's no way of saying just how long I slept, but I'd guess it was more than an hour and less than two.

Maybe a noise outside woke me. Maybe my nap had simply run its course. But I've always thought it was the voice itself; I must have heard and recognized it on some subconscious level.

Whatever the cause, I opened my eyes. And stared. And blinked furiously and stared again.

IT WAS a few minutes after five when Ruth got back. I'd very nearly worn out the rug by then, pacing back and forth across its bare threads, scuttling periodically to the phone, then backing away from it without so much as lifting the receiver. At five o'clock the TV news came on but I was too tautly wired to watch it and could barely pay attention while a beaming chap rattled on and on about something hideous that had just happened in Morocco. (Or Lebanon. One of those places.)

Then Ruth's step on the stairs and her key in the lock, and I opened the door before she could turn the key and she popped energetically inside and spun around to lock the door, the words already spilling from her lips. She seemed to have no end of things to tell me about the weather outside and the facilities at the public library and the service for J. Francis Flaxford, but she might as well have been speaking whatever they speak in Morocco (or Lebanon) for all the attention I was able to pay her.

I cut in right in the middle of a sentence. "Our fat friend," I said. "Was he there?"

"No, I don't think so. Not at the service and not at Pandora's. That's a pretty crummy bar, incidentally. It—"

"So you didn't see him."

"No, but—"

"Well," I said. "*I* did."

Chapter Nine

"AN ACTOR!"

"An actor," I agreed. "I slept through most of the movie. I was just lucky that I woke up for his scene. There he was, looking back over the seat of his cab and asking James Garner where he wanted to go. *'Where to, Mac?'* I think that was the very line I came in on, word for precious word."

"And you recognized him just like that?"

"No question about it. It was the same man. The picture was filmed fifteen years ago and he's not as young as he used to be, but who do you know that is? Same face, same voice, same build. He's put on a few pounds since then, but who hasn't? Oh, it's him, all right. You'd know him if you saw him. As an actor, I mean. I must have watched him in hundreds of movies and TV shows, playing a cabdriver or a bank teller or a minor hoodlum."

"What's his name?"

"Who knows? I'm rotten at trivia. And they didn't run the list of credits at the end of the movie. I sat there waiting, and of course Garner never happened to hail that particular cab a second time, not that I really expected him to, and then there were no credits at the end. I guess they cut them a lot of the time when they show movies on television. And they don't always have them in the first place, do they?"

"I don't think so. Would he be listed anyway? If he didn't say more than *'Where to, Mac?'* "

"Oh, he had other lines, maybe half a dozen lines. You know, talking about the weather and the traffic, doing the typical New York cabbie number. Or at least what Hollywood thinks the typical New York cabbie number ought to be. Did a cabdriver ever say *'Where to, Mac?'* to you?"

"No, but not that many people call me Mac. It's funny. You said he seemed familiar to you and you couldn't figure out where you saw him before."

"I saw him on the screen. Over and over. That's why even his voice was familiar." I frowned. "That's how I recognized him, Ruth. But how in the hell did he recognize me? I'm not an actor. Except in the sense that all the world's a stage. Why would an actor happen to know that Bernie Rhodenbarr is a burglar?"

"I don't know. Maybe—"

"Rodney."

"Huh?"

"Rod's an actor."

"So?"

"Actors know each other, don't they?"

"Do they? I don't know. I suppose some of them do. Do burglars know each other?"

"That's different."

"Why is it different?"

"Burglary is solitary work. Acting is a whole lot of people on a stage or in front of a camera. Actors work with each other. Maybe he worked with this guy."

"I suppose it's possible."

"And Rodney knows me. From the poker game."

"But he doesn't know you're a burglar."

"Well, I didn't think he did. But maybe he does."

"Only if he's been reading the New York papers lately. You think Rodney happened to know you were a burglar and then he told this actor, and the other actor decided you'd be just the person to frame for murder, and just to round things out you went from the murder scene to Rodney's apartment."

"Oh."

"Just like that."

"It does call for more than the usual voluntary suspension of disbelief," I admitted. "But there are actors all over this thing."

"Two of them, and only one of them's all over it."

"Flaxford was connected with the theater. Maybe that's the connection between him and the actor who roped me in. He was a producer, and maybe he had a disagreement with this actor—"

"Who decided to kill him and set up a burglar to take a fall for him."

"I keep blowing up balloons and you keep sticking pins in them."

"It's just that I think we should work with what we know, Bernie. It doesn't matter how this man found you, not right now it doesn't. What matters is how you and I are going to find him. Did you notice the name of the picture?"

"*The Man in the Middle*. And it's about a corporate takeover, not a homosexual *ménage à trois* as you might have thought. Starring James Garner and Shan Willson, and I could tell you the names of two or three others but none of them were our friend. It was filmed in 1962 and whoever the droll chap is who does the TV listings in the *Times*, he thinks the plot is predictable but the performances are spritely. That's a word you don't hear much anymore."

"You wouldn't want to hear it too often."

"I guess not," I said. She picked up the phone book and I told her she'd want the Yellow Pages. "I thought of that," I said. "Call one of those film rental places and see if they can come up with a print of the picture. But they'll be closed at this hour, won't they?"

She gave me a funny look and asked me what channel the movie had been on.

"Channel 9."

"Is that WPIX?"

"WOR."

"Right." She closed the phone book, dialed a number. "You weren't serious about renting the film just so we could see who was in it, were you?"

"Well, sort of."

"Someone at the channel should have a cast list. They must get calls like this all the time."

"Oh."

"Is there any coffee, Bernie?"

"I'll get you some."

It took more than one call. Evidently the people at WOR were used to getting nutty calls from movie buffs, and since such buffs constituted the greater portion of their audience they were prepared to cater to them. But it seemed that the cast list which accompanied the film only concerned itself with featured performers. Our Typical New York Cabdriver, with his half-dozen typical lines, did not come under that heading.

They kept Ruth on the phone for a long time anyway because the fellow she talked to was certain that an associate of his would be sure to know who played the cabdriver in *Man in the Middle*. The associate in question was evidently a goldmine of such information. But this associate was out grabbing a sandwich, and Ruth was understandably reluctant to supply a callback number, and so they chatted and killed time until the guy came back and got on the line. Of course he didn't remember who played the cabdriver, although he did remember some bit taking place in a cab, and then Ruth tried to describe the pear-shaped man, which I felt was slightly nervy, since she'd never seen him, either live or on film. But she echoed my description accurately enough and the conversation went on for a bit and she thanked him very much and hung up.

"He says he knows exactly who I mean," she reported, "but he can't remember his name."

"Sensational."

"But he found out the film was a Paramount release."

"So?"

Los Angeles Information gave her the number for Paramount Pictures. It was three hours earlier out there so that people were still at their desks, except for the ones who hadn't come back from lunch yet. Ruth went through channels until she found somebody who told her that the cast list for a picture more than ten years old would be in the inactive files. So Paramount referred her to the Academy of Motion Picture Arts and Sciences, and L.A. Information came through with the number, and Ruth placed the call. Someone at the Academy told her the information was on file and she was welcome to drive over and look it up for herself, which would have been a time-consuming process, the drive amounting to some three thousand miles. They gave her a hard time until she mentioned that she was David Merrick's secretary. I guess that was a good name to mention.

"He's looking it up," she told me, covering the mouthpiece with her hand.

"I thought you never lie."

"I occasionally tell an expeditious untruth."

"How does that differ from a barefaced lie?"

"It's a subtle distinction." She started to add something to that but someone on the other side of the continent began talking and she said things like *yes* and *uh-huh* and scribbled furiously on the cover of the phone book. Then she conveyed Mr. Merrick's thanks and replaced the receiver.

To me she said, "Which cabdriver?"

"Huh?"

"There are two cabdrivers listed in the complete cast list. There's one called Cabby and another called Second Cabby." She looked at the notes she had made. "Paul Couhig is Cabby and Wesley Brill is Second Cabby. Which one do you suppose we want?"

"Wesley Brill."

"You recognize the name?"

"No, but he was the last cabby in the picture. That would put him second rather than first, wouldn't it?"

"Unless when you saw him he was coming back for an encore."

I grabbed the directory. There were no Couhigs in Manhattan, Paul or otherwise. There were plenty of Brills but no Wesley.

"It could be a stage name," she suggested.

"Would a bit player bother with a stage name?"

"Nobody sets out to be a bit player, not at the beginning of a career. Anyway, there might have been another actor with his real name and he would have had to pick out something else for himself."

"Or he might have an unlisted phone. Or live in Queens, or—"

"We're wasting time." She picked up the phone again. "SAG'll have addresses for both of them. Couhig and Brill." She asked the Information operator for the number of the Screen Actors Guild, which saved me from having to ask what SAG was. Then she dialed another ten numbers and asked someone how to get in touch with our two actor friends. She wasn't bothering to be David Merrick's secretary this time. Evidently it wasn't necessary. She waited a few minutes, then made circles in the air with her pen. I gave the phone book back to her and she scribbled some more on its cover. "It's Brill," she said. "You were right."

"Don't tell me they described him for you."

"He has a New York agent. That's all they would do is give me the agents' names and numbers, and Couhig's represented by the West Coast William Morris office and Brill has an agent named Peter Alan Martin."

"And Martin's here in New York?"

"Uh-huh. He has an Oregon 5 telephone number."

"I suppose actors would tend to be on the same coast as their agents."

"It does sound logical," she agreed. She began dialing, listened for a few minutes, then blew a raspberry into the phone and hung up. "He's gone for the day," she said. "I got one of those answering machines. I hate the damn things."

"Everyone does."

"If my agent had a machine instead of a service I'd get a new agent."

"I didn't know you had an agent."

She colored. "If I had one. If we had some ham we could have ham and eggs if we had some eggs."

"We've still got some eggs. In the fridge."

"Bernie—"

"I know." I looked again in the phone book. No Wesley Brill, but there were a couple of Brill, W's. The first two numbers answered and reported that there was no Wesley there. The third and last went unanswered, but it was in Harlem and it seemed unlikely that he'd live there. And telephone listings with initials are almost always women trying to avoid obscene calls.

"We can find out if he has an unlisted number," Ruth suggested. "Information'll tell you that."

"An actor with an unlisted number? I suppose it's possible. But even if we find out that he does, what good will it do us?"

"None, I suppose."

"Then the hell with it."

"Right."

"We know who he is," I said. "That's the important thing. In the morning we can call his agent and find out where he lives. What's really significant is that we've found a place to start. That's the one thing we didn't have before. If the police kick the door in an hour from now it'd be a slightly different story from if they'd kicked it in two hours ago. I wouldn't be at a complete dead end, see. I'd have more than a cockeyed story about a round-shouldered fat man with brown eyes. I'd have a name to go with the description."

"And then what would happen?"

"They'd put me in jail and throw the key away," I said. "But nobody's going to kick the door in. Don't worry about a thing, Ruth."

She went around the corner to a deli and picked up sandwiches and beer, stopped at a liquor store for a bottle of Teacher's. I'd asked her to pick up the booze, but by the time she came back with everything I'd decided not to have any. I had one beer with dinner and nothing else.

Afterward we sat on the couch and drank coffee. She had a little Scotch in hers. I didn't. She asked to see my burglar tools and I showed them to her, and she asked the name and function of each item.

"Burglar tools," she said. "It's illegal to have them in your possession, isn't it?"

"You can go to jail for it."

"Which ones did you use to open the locks for this apartment?" I showed her and explained the process. "I think it's remarkable," she said, and gave a delicious little shiver. "Who taught you how to do it?"

"Taught myself."

"Really?"

"More or less. Oh, once I was really into it I got books on locksmithing, and then I took a mail-order course in it from an outfit in Ohio. You know, I wonder if anybody but burglars ever sign up for those courses. I knew a guy in prison who took one of those courses with a correspondence college and they sent him a different lock every month by mail with complete instructions on how to open it. He would just sit there in his cell and practice with the lock for hours on end."

"And the prison authorities let him do this?"

"Well, the idea was that he was learning a trade. They're supposed to encourage that sort of thing in prison. Actually the trade he was learning was burglary, of course, and it was a big step up for him from holding up filling stations, which was his original field of endeavor."

"I guess there's more money in burglary."

"There often is, but the main consideration was violence. Not that he ever shot anybody but somebody took a shot at him once and he decided that stealing was a safer and saner proposition if you did it when nobody was home."

"So he took a course and became an expert."

I shrugged. "Let's just say he took the course. I don't know if he became an expert or not. There's only so much you can teach a person, through the mails or face to face. The rest has to be inside him."

"In the hands?"

"In the hands and in the heart." I felt myself blushing at the phrase. "Well, it's true. When I was twelve years old I taught myself how to open the bathroom door. You could lock it from inside by pressing this button on the doorknob and then the door could be opened from the inside but not from the outside. So that nobody would walk in on you while you were on the toilet or in the tub. The usual privacy lock. But of course you can press the button on the inside and then close the door from the outside and then you've locked yourself out of it."

"So?"

"So my kid sister did something along those lines, except what she did was lock herself in and then just sit there and cry because she couldn't turn the knob. My mother called the Fire Department and they took the lock apart and rescued her. What's so funny?"

"Any other kid who went through that would decide to become a fireman. But you decided to become a burglar."

"All I decided was I wanted to know how to open that lock. I tried using a screwdriver blade to get a purchase on the bolt and snick it back, but it didn't have the flexibility. I could almost manage it with a table knife, and then I thought to use one of those plastic calendars insurance men pass out that you keep in your wallet, you know, all twelve months at a glance, and it was perfect. I figured out how to loid that lock without even having heard of the principle involved."

"Loid?"

"As in celluloid. Any time you've got a lock that you can lock without a key, you know, just by drawing the door shut, then you've got a lock that can be loided. It may be hard or easy depending on how the door and jamb fit together, but it's not going to be impossible."

"It's fascinating," she said, and she gave that little shivery shudder again. I went on talking about my earliest experiences with locks and the special thrill I'd always found in opening them, and she seemed as eager to hear all this as I was to talk about it. I told her about the first time I let myself into a neighbor's apartment, going in one afternoon when nobody was home, taking some cold cuts from the refrigerator and bread from the bread drawer, making a sandwich and eating it and putting everything back the way I'd found it before letting myself out.

"The big thing for you was opening locks," she said.

"Opening locks and sneaking inside. Right."

"The stealing came later, then."

"Unless you count sandwiches. But it didn't take long before I was stealing. Once you're inside a place it's a short step to figuring out that it might make sense to leave with more money than you brought with you. Opening doors is a kick, but part of the kick comes from the possibility of profit on the other side of the door."

"And the danger?"

"I suppose that's part of it."

"Bernie? Tell me what it's like."

"Burglary?"

"Uh-huh." Her face was quite intense now, especially around the eyes, and there was a thin film of perspiration on her upper lip. I put a hand on her leg. A muscle in her upper thigh twitched like a plucked string.

"Tell me how it feels," she said.

I moved my hand to and fro. "It feels very nice," I said.

"You know what I mean. What's it like to open a door and sneak into somebody else's place?"

"Exciting."

"It must be." Her tongue flicked at her lower lip.

"Scary?"

"A little."

"It would have to be. Is the excitement, uh, sexual?"

"Depends on who you find in the apartment." I laughed a

hearty laugh. "Just a joke. I suppose there's a sexual element. It's obvious enough on a symbolic level, isn't it?" My hand moved as I talked, to and fro, to and fro. "Tickling all the right tumblers," I went on. "Stroking here and there, then ever so gently easing the door open, slipping inside little by little."

"Yes—"

"Of course your crude type of burglar who uses a pry bar or just plain kicks the door in, he'd be representative of a more direct approach to sex, wouldn't he?"

She pouted. "You're joking with me."

"Just a little."

"I never met a burglar before, Bernie. I'm curious to know what it's like."

Her eyes looked blue now and utterly guileless. I put a finger under her chin, tipped her head up, placed a little kiss upon the tip of her nose. "You'll know," I told her.

"Huh?"

"In a couple of hours," I said, "you'll get to see for yourself."

IT MADE perfect sense to me. She was remarkably good at getting people to tell her things over the phone, and maybe she could worm Wesley Brill's address out of his agent first thing in the morning, but why wait so long? And why chance the agent's passing the word to Wesley? Or, if the agent was in on the whole thing, why set his teeth on edge?

On the other hand, Peter Alan Martin's office was located on Sixth Avenue and Sixteenth Street, and if there was anything easier than knocking off an office building after hours I didn't know what it was. At the very least I'd walk out of the building with Brill's address a few hours earlier than we'd get it otherwise, and without

arousing suspicions. And if I got lucky—well, it had the same attraction as any burglary. You didn't know what you might find,
and it could always turn out to be more than you'd hoped for.

"But you'll be out in the open," Ruth said. "People might see
you."

"I'll be disguised."

Her face brightened. "We could get some makeup. Maybe Rod
has some around. I'll make you up. Maybe a false moustache for a
start."

"I tried a real moustache this afternoon and I wasn't crazy
about it. And makeup just makes a person look as though he's
wearing makeup, and that's the sort of thing that draws attention
instead of discouraging it. Wait here a minute."

I went to the closet, got the wig and cap, took them into the
bathroom and used the mirror to adjust them for the best effect. I
came out and posed for Ruth. She was properly appreciative, and
I bowed theatrically, and when I did so the cap and wig fell on
the rug in front of me. Whereupon she laughed a little more
boisterously than I felt the situation absolutely required.

"Not that funny," I said.

"Oh, nonsense. It was hysterical. A couple of bobby pins will
make sure that doesn't happen. It could be embarrassing if your
hair fell off on the street."

Nothing happened last night, I thought. But I didn't say anything. I hadn't mentioned that I'd gone out on my own and I felt
it would be awkward to bring it up now.

It was around nine when we left the apartment. I had my ring
of tools in my pocket along with my rubber gloves and a roll of
adhesive tape I'd found in the medicine cabinet; I didn't think I'd

have to break any windows, but adhesive tape is handy if you do and I hadn't cased Martin's office and didn't know what to expect. Ruth had found some bobby pins lurking in the bottom of her bag and she used them to attach the blond wig to my own hair. I could bow clear to the floor now and not worry about dislodging the wig. Of course I'd lose the cap, and she wanted to pin the cap to the wig as well, but I drew the line there.

Outside the door I took Rod's spare keys from her and locked all three locks, then gave them back to her. She looked at them for a moment before dropping them back into her bag. "You opened all those locks," she said. "Without keys."

"I'm a talented lad."

"You must be."

We didn't run into anyone on the way out of the building. Outside the air was fresh and clear and not a touch warmer than it had been the night before. I almost said as much until I remembered I hadn't been out the night before as far as she was concerned. She said it must feel good to be outside after spending two days cooped up, and I said yeah, it sure did, and she said I must be nervous being on the streets with every cop in the city gunning for me, which was something of an exaggeration, and I said yeah, I sure was, but not too nervous, and she took my arm and we headed north and east.

It was a lot safer with her along. Anybody looking at us saw a guy and a girl walking arm in arm, and when that's what meets your eye it doesn't occur to you to wonder if you're eyeballing a notorious fugitive from justice. I was able to relax a good deal more than I had the past night. I think she was edgy at first, but by the time we'd walked a few blocks she was completely at ease and said she couldn't wait until we were inside the agent's office.

I said, "What you mean *we*, kemosabe?"

"You and me, Tonto. Who else?"

"Uh-uh," I said. "Not a chance. I'm the burglar, remember? You're the trusted confederate. You stay on the outskirts and guard the horses."

She pouted. "Not fair. You have all the fun."

"Rank has its privileges."

"Two heads are better than one, Bernie. And four hands are better than two, and if we're both checking Martin's office things'll go faster."

I reminded her about too many cooks. She was still protesting when we reached the corner of Sixteenth and Sixth. I figured out which was Martin's building and spotted a Riker's coffee shop diagonally across the street from it. "You'll wait right there," I told her, "in one of those cute little booths with a cup of what will probably not turn out to be the best coffee you ever tasted."

"I don't want any coffee."

"Maybe an English muffin along with it if you feel the need."

"I'm not hungry."

"Or a prune Danish. They're renowned for their prune Danish."

"Really?"

"How do I know? You can hold up lanterns in the window. One if by land, two if by sea, and Ruth Hightower'll be on the opposite shore. What's the matter?"

"Nothing."

"*Two If By Sea.* That's the show Rod's in, did you know that? Anyway, I'll be on the opposite shore, and I won't be terribly long. Get in and get out, quick as a bunny. That's my policy."

"I see."

"But only in burglary. It's not my policy in all areas of human endeavor."

"Huh? Oh."

I felt lighthearted, even a little light-headed. I gave her a comradely kiss and steered her toward the Riker's, then squared my shoulders and prepared to do battle.

Chapter Ten

THE building was only a dozen stories high, but the man who built it had probably thought of it as a skyscraper at the time. It was that old, a once-white structure festooned with ornamental ironwork and layered with decades of grime. They don't build them like that anymore and you really can't blame them.

I looked the place over from across the street and didn't see anything that bothered me. Most of the streetside offices were dark. Only a few had lights on—lawyers and accountants working late, cleaning women tidying desks and emptying trash baskets and mopping floors. In the narrow marble-floored lobby, a white-haired black man in maroon livery sat at a desk reading a newspaper, which he held at arm's length. I watched him for a few minutes. No one entered the building, but one man emerged from the elevator and approached the desk. He bent over it for a moment, then straightened up and continued on out of the building, heading uptown on Sixth Avenue.

I slipped into a phone booth on the corner and tried not to pay attention to the way it smelled. I called Peter Alan Martin's office and hung up when the machine answered. If you do that within seven seconds or so you get your dime back. I must have taken eight seconds because Ma Bell kept my money.

When the traffic light changed I trotted across the street. The attendant looked up without interest as I made my way through the revolving doors. I gave him my Number 3 smile, warm but impersonal, and let my eyes have a quick peek at the building directory on the wall while my feet carried me over to his desk. He moved a hand to indicate the ledger and the yellow pencil stub I was to use to sign my name in it. I wrote *T. J. Powell* under Name, *Hubbell Corp.* under Firm, *441* under Room, and *9:25* under Time In. I could have written the Preamble to the Constitution for all the attention the old man gave it, and why not? He was an autograph collector and not a hell of a lot more, a deterrent for people who deterred easily. He'd been posted in the lobby of a fifth-rate office building where the tenants probably had an annual turnover rate of thirty percent. Industrial espionage was hardly likely to occur here, and if the old man kept the junkies from carting off typewriters, then he was earning the pittance they paid him.

The elevator had been inexpertly converted to self-service some years back. It was a rickety old cage and it took its time getting up to the fourth floor, which was where I left it. Martin's office was on six, and I didn't really think my friend in the lobby would abandon his tabloid long enough to see if I went to the floor I'd signed in for, but when you're a professional you tend to do things the right way whether you have to or not. I took the fire stairs up two flights—and they were unusually steep flights at that—and found the agent's office at the far end of the corridor. There were lights burning in only two of the offices I passed, one belonging to a CPA, the other to a firm called Notions Unlimited. No sound came from the accountant's office, but a radio in Notions Unlimited was tuned to a classical music station, and over what was probably a Vivaldi chamber work a girl with an Haute Bronx accent was saying, ". . . told him he had a lot to learn, and do you know what he said to that? You're not going to believe this . . ."

The door to Peter Alan Martin's office was of blond maple with a large pane of frosted glass set into it. The glass had all three of his names on it in black capitals, and TALENT REPRESENTATIVE underneath them. The lettering had been done some time ago and needed freshening up, but then the whole building needed that sort of touch-up work and you knew it wasn't ever going to get it. I could tell without opening the door that Martin wasn't much of an agent and Brill couldn't have much of a career these days. On the outside the building still retained an air of faded grandeur, but in here all of the grandeur had faded away.

The door's single lock had both a snap lock and a deadbolt, and Martin had taken the trouble to turn his key in the lock and put the deadbolt to work. It was hard to figure out why, because locking a door like that is like fencing a cornfield to keep the crows out. Any idiot could simply break the glass and reach inside, and I had adhesive tape that would enable me to break the glass without raising the dead; a few strips crisscrossed on the pane would keep the clatter and tinkle to a minimum.

A broken pane of glass is a calling card, though, especially if they find it with tape on it. Since I didn't expect to steal anything,

I had the opportunity to get in and out without anyone ever knowing I'd existed. So I took the time to pick the lock, and there was precious little time involved. I knocked off the deadbolt easily, and loiding the snap lock was more than easy. There was a good quarter-inch of air between the wooden door and its wooden jamb, and a child with a butter spreader could have let himself in.

"What's it like, Bernie?"

Well, there was a little excitement in turning the knob and easing the door open, then slipping inside and closing the door and locking up. I had my pencil light with me but I left it in my pocket and switched on the overhead fluorescents right away. A little flashlight winking around in that office might have looked strange from outside, but this way it was just another office with the lights on and I was just another poor bastard working late.

I moved around quickly, taking the most perfunctory sort of inventory. An old wooden desk, a gray steel steno desk with typewriter, a long table, a couple of chairs. I got the feel of the layout while establishing that there were no corpses tucked in odd places, then went over to the window and looked out. I could see Riker's but couldn't look inside. I wondered if Ruth was at a front table and if she might be looking up at my very window. But I didn't wonder about this for very long.

I checked my watch. Nine thirty-six.

Martin's office was shabby and cluttered. One entire wall was covered with dark brown cork tiles, which had been inexpertly cemented to it. Thumbtacks and pushpins held glossy photographs in place. The greater portion of these photos showed women, who in turn showed the greater portion of themselves. Most of them showed their legs, many showed their breasts, and every one of them flashed a savage mechanical smile. I thought of Peter Alan Martin sitting at his cluttered desk and gazing up at all those teeth and I felt a little sorry for him.

There were a few head-and-shoulders shots in among the sea of tits and legs, a couple of male faces in the crowd. But I didn't see the face I was looking for.

Next to the white touchtone phone on the desk stood a Rolodex wheel of phone numbers and addresses. I flipped through it and found Wesley Brill's card. This didn't really come as a surprise, but all the same I felt a little thrill when I actually located what I was looking for. I tried a couple of Martin's Flair pens, finally found one that worked, and copied down *Wesley Brill, Hotel Cumberland, 326 West 58th, 541-7255.* (I don't know why I wrote down his name. I don't know why I wrote down anything, come to think of it, because all I had to do was remember the name of the hotel and the rest would be in the phone book. Listen, nobody's perfect.)

I put my rubber gloves on at about this point and wiped the surfaces I remembered touching, not that any of them seemed likely to take a print and not that anyone would be looking for prints in the first place. I checked the Rolodex for Flaxford, not really expecting to find his name, and was not vastly surprised when it wasn't there.

There were three old green metal filing cabinets on the opposite side of the window from the cork wall. I gave them a quick look-through and found Brill's file. All it held was a sheaf of several dozen 8 by 10 glossies. If Martin had any correspondence with or about Brill he either threw it out or kept it elsewhere.

But it was the pictures that interested me. Only when I saw them did I know for certain that Wesley Brill was the man who had set me up for a murder rap. Until then there was still some room for doubt. All those long-distance phone calls had had us operating in something of a vacuum, but here was Brill in living black and white and there was no doubt about it. I flipped through the pictures and picked out a composite shot, half a dozen head-and-shoulders pics arranged to show various facial expressions and attitudes. I knew it wouldn't be missed—mostly likely the whole file wouldn't have been missed, and possibly the entire filing cabinet that contained it—and I folded it twice and put it in a pocket.

Martin's desk wasn't locked. I went through it quickly, mechanically, without finding anything to tell me much about Wesley Brill. I did come upon a mostly-full pint of blended whiskey in the bottom drawer and an unopened half-pint of Old Mr. Boston mint-flavored gin snuggled up next to it. Both of these were infinitely resistible. In the wide center drawer I found an envelope with some cash in it, eighty-five dollars in fives and tens. I took a five and two tens to cover expenses, put the rest back, closed the drawer, then changed my mind and opened it again and scooped up the rest of the money, leaving the empty envelope in the drawer. Now if I left any evidence of my presence, if the clutter I left behind struck him as different from the clutter he'd left there himself, he'd simply think it was the work of some hot-prowl artist who'd made off with his mad money.

(Then why was I disguising my presence in every other respect? Ah, you've spotted an inconsistency, haven't you? All right, I'll tell you why I took the eighty-five bucks. I've never believed in overlooking cash. That's why.)

But I *was* careful to overlook what I found in the top left-hand drawer. It was a tiny little revolver with a two-inch barrel and pearlized grips, and tiny or not it looked very menacing. I leaned into the drawer to sniff intelligently at the barrel the way they're always doing on television. Then they state whether or not the gun's been fired recently. All I could state was that I smelled metal and mineral oil and what you usually smell in a musty desk drawer, a drawer which I was now very happy to close once I got my nose out of it.

Guns make me nervous, and you'd be surprised how many times a burglar will run across one. I only once had one pointed at me and that was one I've mentioned, the gun of good old Carter Sandoval, but I've found them in drawers and on night tables and, more than once, tucked beneath a pillow. People buy the hateful things to shoot burglars with, or at least that's what they tell themselves, and then they wind up shooting themselves or each other accidentally or on purpose.

A lot of burglars steal guns automatically, either because they have a use for them or because it's a cinch to get fifty or a hundred dollars for a nice untraceable handgun. And I knew one fellow who specialized in suburban homes who always took guns with him so that the next burglar to hit that place wouldn't be risking a bullet. He took every gun he encountered and always dropped them down the nearest sewer. "We have to look out for each other," he told me.

I've never stolen a gun and I didn't even contemplate stealing Martin's. I don't even like to touch the damned things and I closed the drawer without touching this one.

At nine fifty-seven I let myself out of the office. The corridor was empty. Faint strains of Mozart wafted my way from the Notions Unlimited office. I wasted a minute relocking the door, though I could have let him figure he'd forgotten to lock up.

Anybody with Peter Alan Martin's taste in booze probably greeted the dawn with a fairly spotty memory of the previous day.

I even walked down to the fourth floor before I rang for the elevator. Nobody was home at Hubbell Corp. I rode the elevator to the lobby, found my name in the ledger—three people had come in since my arrival, and one of them had left already. I penciled in *10 p.m.* under Time Out and wished the old man in the wine-colored uniform a pleasant evening.

"They all the same," he said. "Good nights and bad nights, all one and the same to me."

I CAUGHT Ruth's eye from Riker's doorway. The place was fairly deserted, a couple of cabbies at the counter, two off-duty hookers in the back booth. Ruth put some coins on her table next to her coffee cup and hurried to join me. "I was starting to worry," she said.

"Not to worry."

"You were gone a long time."

"Half an hour."

"Forty minutes. Anyway, it seemed like hours. What happened?"

She took my arm and I told her about it as we walked. I was feeling very good. I hadn't accomplished anything that remarkable but I felt a great sense of exhilaration. Everything was starting to go right now, I could feel it, and it was a nice feeling.

"He's in a hotel in the West Fifties," I told her. "Just off Columbus Circle, near the Coliseum. That's why he didn't have a listed phone. I never heard of the hotel and I have a feeling it's not in the same class with the Sherry-Netherland. In fact I think our Mr. Brill has had hard times lately. He's got a loser for an agent, that's for sure. Most of Peter Alan Martin's clients are ladies who came in third in a county-wide beauty contest a whole lot of years ago. I think he's the kind of agent you call when you want someone to come out of the cake at a bachelor party. Do they still have that sort of thing?"

"What sort of thing?"

"Girls popping out of cakes."

"You're asking me? How would I know?"

"That's a point."

"I never popped out of a cake myself. Or attended a bachelor party."

"Then you wouldn't want Martin to represent you. I wonder why he's representing Brill. The guy's had tons of work over the years. Here, you'll recognize him." We moved under a street light and I unfolded the composite sheet for her. "You must have seen him hundreds of times."

"Oh," she said. "Of course I have. Movies, TV."

"Right."

"I can't think where offhand but he's definitely a familiar face. I can even sort of hear his voice. He was in—I can't think exactly what he was in, but—"

"*Man in the Middle*," I suggested. "Jim Garner, Shan Willson, Wes Brill."

"Right."

"So how come he's on the skids? He's got two last names, his agent's got three first names, and he's living in some dump across from the Coliseum and consorting with known criminals. Why?"

"That's one of the things you'll want to ask him tomorrow."

"One, of several things."

We walked a little farther in silence. Then she said, "It must have been a new experience for you, Bernie. Letting yourself into his office and not stealing anything."

"Well, when I first started my criminal career all I stole was a sandwich. And I haven't stolen anything from Rod outside of a little Scotch and a couple cans of soup."

"Sounds as though you're turning over a new leaf."

"Don't count on it. Because I did steal something from Whatsisname. Martin."

"The photograph? I don't think that counts."

"Plus eighty-five dollars. That must count." And I went on to tell her about the money in the desk drawer.

"My God," she said.

"What's the matter?"

"You really *are* a burglar."

"No kidding. What did you think I was?"

She shrugged. "I guess I'm terribly naive. I keep forgetting that you actually steal things. You were in that man's office and there was some money there so you automatically took it."

I had a clever answer handy but I left it alone. Instead I said, "Does it bother you?"

"I wouldn't say that it bothers me. Why should it bother me?"

"I don't know."

"I guess it confuses me."

"I suppose that's understandable."

"But I don't think it bothers me."

We didn't talk much the rest of the way home. When we crossed Fourteenth Street I took her hand and she let me keep it the rest of the way, until we got to the building and she used her key on the downstairs door. The key didn't fit perfectly and it took her about as long to unlock the door as it had taken me to open it without a key. I said as much to her while we climbed the stairs, and she laughed. After we'd climbed three of the four flights she walked up to 4-F and started to poke a key in the lock.

"It won't fit," I said.

"Huh?"

"Wrong apartment. That one's unfit for military service."

"What?"

"Four-F. The draft classification. We're looking for five-R, remember?"

"Oh, for God's sake," she said. Her face reddened. "I was thinking I was at my place. On Bank Street."

"You're in the fourth floor front?"

"Well, fourth floor at the top of the stairs. There are four apartments to a floor; it's not as narrow a building as this one." We walked to the final flight of stairs and began climbing them. "I'm glad no one opened the door while we were there. It would have been embarrassing."

"Don't worry about it now."

In front of Rod's apartment she fished her keys out again, paused for a moment, then turned and deliberately dropped them back into her bag.

"I seem to have misplaced my keys," she said.

"Come on, Ruth."

"Let's see you open it without them. You can do it, can't you?"

"Sure, but what's the point?"

"I guess I'd like to see you do it."

"It's silly," I said. "Suppose someone happens to come along and sees me standing there playing locksmith. It's an unnecessary risk. And these locks are tricky. Well, the Medeco is, anyhow. It can be a bitch to open."

"You managed before, didn't you?"

"Sure, but—"

"I already fed the cats." I turned and stared at her. "Esther and Mordecai. I already fed them."

"Oh," I said.

"This afternoon, on my way back here. I filled their water dish and left them plenty of dried food."

"I see."

"I think it would excite me to watch you open the locks. I told you I felt confused about the whole thing. Well, I do. I think watching you unlock the locks, uh, I think it would get me, uh, hot."

"Oh."

I took my ring of picks out of my pocket.

"I suppose this is all very perverted of me," she said. She put an arm around my waist, leaned her hot little body against mine. "Kinky and all."

"Probably," I said.

"Does it bother you?"

"I think I can learn to live with it," I said. And went to work on those locks.

QUITE a while later she said, "Well, it looks as though I was right. I'm a kinkier bitch than I realized." She yawned richly and snuggled up close. I ran a hand lazily over her body, memorizing the contours of hip and thigh, the secret planes and valleys. My heart was beating normally again, more or less. I lay with my eyes closed and listened to the muffled hum of traffic in the streets below.

She said, "Bernie? You have wonderful hands."

"I should have been a surgeon."

"Oh, do that some more, it's divine. No wonder all the locks open for you. I don't think you really need all those curious implements after all. Just stroke the locks a little and they get all soft and mushy inside and open right up."

"You're a wee bit flaky, aren't you?"

"Just a wee bit. But you have got the most marvelous hands. I wish I had hands like yours."

"There's nothing wrong with your hands, baby."

"Really?"

And her hands began to move.

"Hey," I said.

"Something the matter?"

"Just what do you think you're doing, lady?"

"Just what do you think I'm doing?"

"Playing with fire."

"Oh?"

The first time had been intense and urgent, even a bit desperate. Now we were slow and lazy and gentle with each other. There was no music on the radio, just the sound of the city below us, but in my head I heard smoky jazz full of blue notes and muted brass. At the end I said *"Ruth Ruth Ruth"* and closed my eyes and died and went to Heaven.

I AWOKE first in the morning. For a moment something was wrong. The ghost of a dream was flickering somewhere behind my closed eyelids and I wanted to catch hold of it and ask it its name. But it was gone, out of reach. I lay still for a moment, taking deep breaths. Then I turned on my side and she was there beside me and for this I was grateful. At first I did nothing but look at her and listen to the even rhythm of her breathing. Then I thought of other things to do, and then I did them.

Eventually we got out of bed, took our turns in the bathroom, and put on the clothes we'd thrown off hastily the night before. She made the coffee and burned the toast and we sat down in silence and had breakfast.

There was something wrong with this particular silence. Ray Kirschmann's young partner Loren would have slapped his battered nightstick against his palm and said something inarticulate about vibrations, and maybe that would have been as good an explanation as any. Perhaps I read something in the tilt of her head, the set of her chin. I didn't know exactly what it was but something was not at all right.

I said, "What's the matter, Ruth?"

"Ruth," she said.

"Huh?"

"*Dear Ruth.* That's a play."

"Baby Ruth," I said. "That's a candy bar."

"Ruth Ruth Ruth. You said that last night. And this morning, too. At the very end."

"*You* said 'Sweet fucking shit I'm coming,' but I hadn't planned on throwing it in your face for breakfast. If you don't like your name why don't you change it?"

"I like my name fine."

"Then what's the trouble?"

"Shit. Look, Bernie, if you keep calling me Ruth I'm going to start calling you Roger."

"Huh?"

"As in Armitage."

"Oh," I said. Then my eyes widened a bit and my jaw slackened and I said Oh again, but with a little more conviction, and she gave a slow nod.

"Your name isn't Ruth Hightower."

"Too true." She averted her eyes. "Well, *you* were calling yourself Roger and I knew that wasn't your name and I thought we ought to start on an equal footing. And then we got it straightened out who you were and it just seemed easier for me to go on being Ruth. There was never a convenient time to tell you."

"Until now."

"If you're going to murmur a name into my ear at intimate moments I'd just as soon you got the name right."

"I guess I can understand that. Well?"

"Well what?"

"Well, what's your name? Take plenty of time, kid. Make sure you come up with one that'll sound nice in a husky whisper."

"That's not nice."

"Not nice! Here I am feeling like an utter zip, cooing some alias into your pink shell-like ear, and you tell me I'm not nice?" I turned her face so that I could see her eyes. There were tears welling up in their corners. "Hey," I said. "Hey, come on now."

She blinked furiously but the tears did not go away. She blinked some more, then erased the tears with the back of her hand. "I'm all right," she said.

"Of course you are."

"My name's Ellie."

"For Eleanor?"

"For Elaine, but Ellie'll do just fine."

"Ellie what? Not Hightower, I don't suppose."

"Ellie Christopher."

"Pretty name."

"Thank you."

"I think it suits you. But then I thought Ruth Hightower suited you pretty well, so who am I to say? What do I know? Is Christopher your married name?"

"No. I took my maiden name back after the divorce."

"What was your husband's name?"

"What's the difference?"

"I don't know."

"Are you angry with me, Bernie?"

"Why should I be angry?"

"You didn't answer my question."

I went on not answering it and finished my coffee, then got to my feet. "We've both got things to do," I said. "I want to go to my apartment."

"I don't know if that's safe."

I didn't either but I didn't feel like talking about it. I couldn't believe the cops would have my place staked out, not at this point, and a phone call would let me know if there was anyone on the premises at the moment. And I really wanted clean clothes, and I had the feeling it would be nice to have my case money on hand. Things were almost ready to come to a head and the five grand I'd tucked away at my place might turn out to be useful.

"Things to do," I said. "You want to go back to your place and change your clothes, freshen up, that sort of thing. And feed your cats."

"I suppose so."

"And empty the catbox and put out fresh kitty litter, all those things. Take the garbage out to the incinerator. The little day-to-day chores that eat up so much of a person's time."

"Bernie—"

"Do you really have cats? Abyssinians? And are their names really Esther and Ahasuerus?"

"Esther and Mordecai."

"There's a lot I don't know about you, isn't there?"

"Not so very damned much. I don't see what you're so thoroughly pissed about."

I didn't either, exactly. But I glared at her anyway.

"Give me a little room, huh? I'm just a neighborhood kid who wandered in one morning to water the plants."

"Well, you don't owe me anything, that's for sure."

"Bernie—"

"I'll meet you at the Childs on Eighth Avenue and Fifty-eighth Street," I said. "That'll be a few doors from his hotel. Do you still want to come along?"

"Of course. And I'll dress up like we said last night? Nothing's changed, Bernie."

I let that pass and looked at my watch. "It's a quarter after ten," I said. "Figure two hours to do everything we have to do plus a margin for error, so that makes what? I'll meet you at the restaurant at twelve thirty. How does that sound?"

"It sounds fine."

I got the wig and cap and she came around and helped me with the bobby pins. I wanted to do it myself but I forced myself to stand still while she poked around there. "If I'm not there by one o'clock," I said, "you can assume I got arrested."

"That's not funny."

"Lots of things aren't. Don't forget to lock up. The streets are full of burglars."

"Bernie—"

"I mean it. It's a jungle out there."

"Bernie—"

"What?"

"Just be careful."

"Oh, I'm always careful," I said, and let myself out.

Chapter Eleven

IN THE taxi heading uptown I thought about Ellie (whom I found myself still thinking of as Ruth) and wondered why I'd gotten so steamed with her. She told me a lie or three, but so what? On balance she'd placed herself in jeopardy to help a total stranger who looked to be a murderer in the bargain. On the strength of her vaunted intuition she'd put herself on the line for me. So what if she kept her name to herself? That seemed like no more than a sensible precaution—if I got nailed by the long arm of the law, I wouldn't be able to drag her into it. Not so long as I didn't know who she was.

And then, when the old animal passions began to churn, she felt bad about the deception. So she told me her name, and everything was right out in the open where it belonged.

So what was my problem?

Well, for openers, I'd been honest with her. And that was a new experience for me. In all my previous relationships with women, a central fact was always kept secret. Whatever else women learned about me—what I ate for breakfast, what I wore to bed, how I like to make love, whether I preferred the smooth or the crunchy peanut butter—they never got to find out what I did for a living. I would explain that I was between positions or that I had a private income or was in investments. Occasionally, if we were not likely to be more to each other than two ships passing in the night, I would equip myself with an interesting business or profession for the duration. At one time or another I had been a magazine illustrator, a neurosurgeon, a composer of modern classical music, a physical education instructor, a stockbroker, and an Arizona land developer.

And I'd always been comfortable playing one of these roles. I'd always told myself that I did this sort of thing because I couldn't afford to let a lady friend know what I really did to support myself, but now I wondered if that was true after all. The more I thought about some of those ladies, the more I got the feeling that they might have reacted pretty much the way Ellie did. Burglary, after all, is the sort of career people are apt to perceive as exciting, the moral implications notwithstanding, and it's been my observation that most women have highly adaptable moral systems.

I'd kept my career a secret because I liked being secretive. Because I didn't want anyone to know me all that well.

With Ruth—no, dammit, Ellie, the woman's name is Ellie, at least until she tells me different—with Ellie, I had no choice. And as a result she'd gotten very close to the real Bernard Rhodenbarr, and at the same time I'd found out what it was like to be intimate with a girl without holding so much of myself in reserve.

And all along I was whispering the wrong name into her ear.

The shoe was on the other foot. That's what it was. All those years of automatically lying to women and now one of them had turned the tables, and I didn't seem to like it much.

I LET the cab drop me right at my door. Not the front door, though, but the service entrance around the corner. I gave the driver one of Peter Alan Martin's limp five-dollar bills and sent him on his way. Easy come, easy go.

I'd been prepared to pick the service entrance lock in broad daylight, that being safer on the balance than slipping past the doorman, but I didn't have to exert any of my special talents because the door was wide open when I got to it. Two enormous men were carrying a small spinet piano through it. I stood aside while they cleared the doorway and went on to load the thing into an unmarked half-ton panel truck. Either they were unlicensed gypsy movers or they'd gone into the business of stealing pianos, which seemed unlikely but by no means impossible, New York being New York. Whatever they were doing was clearly no concern of mine, so I went on into the basement and took the elevator up to the sixteenth floor without attracting any attention whatsoever.

The long narrow corridor was happily empty. I hurried down its length to my very own door, dug my personal key ring out of my pocket, and was about to indulge myself in the unaccustomed luxury of opening a door with a key. Then I got a sudden flash that there was someone in the apartment and cursed myself for not calling up first. I extended a finger to ring my bell, then withdrew it. Either the person inside would just freeze and not answer the bell or he'd yank it open and slap cuffs on me.

I hesitated. I glanced down at my hand, the hand that held the key, and my fingers were trembling. I told myself this was silly and I told my fingers to cut it out and they did. Then I stopped looking at my fingers and looked instead at my lock, or more accurately looked where it had been the last time I'd been home.

There was a neat round hole in the door where my Rabson cylinder belonged. Above it, the Yale springlock the landlord supplied was still in place, but my key wouldn't go into it. I dropped to one knee and had a look at it and it wasn't the original equipment. I could see marks around it where someone had scratched and gouged the door in the process of demolishing the old lock, and now they'd put on a new one to keep people from walking in at will.

I peered through the hole where my sixty-dollar Rabson had been, but the apartment was dark and I couldn't see anything, so I went through the rather absurd ritual of picking my own lock to let myself in. By then I had a feeling I knew what I would find, because it was already clear to me that I'd had more than one set of visitors. The cops might have drilled the Rabson out if they didn't have anyone on hand who could pick it, but they'd have had the super use his key on the other lock, the one that came with the apartment. They certainly wouldn't have employed brute force to kick it in, not after they'd taken the trouble to drill the Rabson. So someone else had come along afterward, someone not inclined to be gentle and painstaking, and that gave me an idea of what my apartment would look like.

But I still wasn't prepared for what lay within. I let myself inside, closing the door and flicking on the light in a single motion, and just like that I was transported to Dresden after the bombing. The place had been turned upside-down and inside-out, and after what had been done to it I couldn't imagine why the super had put a new lock on the door, because no future intruder could have made things any worse than they already were.

Everything I owned was in the middle of the living room floor. Chair cushions had been slashed and the stuffing torn out. Every book had wound up off the shelves and on the floor after having first been taken by the covers and shaken so that anything tucked between its pages would fall out. The wall-to-wall broadloom, imperfectly installed in the first place, had been yanked up so that whatever I might have secreted between it and the padding, or between padding and floor, could be discovered.

God, what a mess! I have always been the neatest of burglars, having nothing but respect for the private property of others, whether I intended to leave that property in their hands or transfer it into my own. The utter lack of consideration my visitors had shown literally sickened me. I had to sit down, but I couldn't find a place to sit. There was not a single inviting surface in that apartment. I managed to put an unupholstered (hence unslashed) chair on its feet and planted myself on it.

What was the point of all this?

The police, of course, would have searched the apartment if only to assure themselves that I wasn't in it. They might have made off with an address book in the hope that it would lead them to possible associates and friends of mine. But the cops, however much they might dislike me for having made them look fairly foolish, would not react by waging total war on my apartment. This carnage was clearly the work of whoever had kicked the door in.

But *why?*

Someone had been looking for something. While no pack of adolescent vandals could have been more destructive, there was too much method to this particular madness for it to be simple vandalism. I was perfectly willing to believe the bastards had enjoyed their work, but all of their efforts had been undertaken with the aim of finding something.

What?

I walked from room to room, trying to figure it out. The little kitchen, never my favorite room at the best of times, had been sacked. I hadn't kept anything in it more valuable than canned ravioli, so there was no reason to waste time looking at the mess. They'd even dumped the contents of the refrigerator, so *mess* was the right word for it

The bedroom had received similar treatment. I ignored the disorder as much as I could and waded through it to the bedroom closet. I'd built a false back wall into that closet just above the overhead shelf, giving myself a space five feet wide and three feet high and some fifteen inches deep that the building's own architect couldn't have found unless he knew what he was looking for. I used that space to stow whatever I might bring back from a midnight shopping spree, holding it there until I'd made arrangements to fence it. I'd had no end of swag tucked away there at one time or another, though never for terribly long. There'd been nothing in it when I was last in the apartment except for a passport and the sort of personal papers other people keep in safe-deposit boxes, but I wanted to see if my visitors, thorough as they'd been, had found my hiding place.

They'd been in the closet, certainly. They had thrown all my clothing onto the bed, pausing only to rip out an occasional jacket lining. But they hadn't found my hiding place and that made me feel a little better. I opened it up, easing the panel out of its moorings, and there were my passport and high school diploma and class picture and sundry treasures. I found myself wishing I'd left a satchel full of emeralds in there just so the bastards could have missed them.

Then I went back to the living room and began sifting through the pile of books. At least half of them had their bindings wholly or partially demolished by the treatment they'd been given. I paid as little attention to this as possible, merely going through the heap until I'd found three individual volumes. These were the book-club edition of *The Guns of August*, the second volume of the three-volume Heritage Press edition of Gibbon's *Decline and Fall of the Roman Empire*, and something called *The Romance of Beekeeping*, which I'd bought because the title struck me as a contradiction in terms. All three books had seen much better days and the cover of the beekeeping book was now attached to the text by a thread and a prayer, but that was all right. I didn't care. I toted the three books into the bedroom and put them on top of my dresser. There was plenty of room there because my visitors had tipped everything that used to be on the top of the dresser onto the floor. Considerate of them to make room for the books.

There was a smallish canvas suitcase in the closet. My leather suitcase had been carved up by a lunatic looking for a secret compartment, I suppose, but the canvas bag was so flimsy that it was obviously hiding nothing. I put my three books in it and added clean clothing from the pile on my bed and the other pile on the bedroom floor. I left myself a change of clothes, packed enough socks and shirts and underwear to last a few days, zipped up the suitcase, then took off the clothes I'd been wearing. I dropped them on the floor along with everything else and went into the bathroom to take a shower.

It was a sloppy shower because my good friends had pulled

down the rod that holds the shower curtain in place. They'd also yanked the towel bars loose from their moorings. Some of these bars are hollow and some people hide things in them. I've never been able to understand why; the stash winds up being hard for its owner to get at, while a prowler or cop can reach it in a second by ripping the bar off the wall.

I've noticed over the years that your average person is not terribly good at hiding things.

Anyway, I had to shower without the benefit of shower curtain, which meant that an awful lot of water wound up on the floor. There were clothes and things there to absorb most of it as it landed. Somehow I just couldn't bring myself to care what happened to the floor or the clothes or the whole apartment, because I was never going to have anything to do with any of them again. I couldn't live in the apartment even if I wanted to, and now I no longer wanted to, so the hell with all of it.

I finished my shower, kicked clothing aside until I found a couple of towels to dry myself with, put on my clean clothes and slid my feet into my best pair of scotch-grain loafers. Then I added a few more things to my suitcase—my own razor, some other toilet articles, a vial of hay fever pills (although it wasn't the season) and a rabbit's foot key chain with no keys on it that I'd given up for lost ages ago. It must have been hiding out in the back of a dresser drawer or something and my guests had located it for me in the process of dumping the drawer. An ill wind that blows no good, said I to myself, and paused in my labors to transfer the rabbit's foot from the suitcase to my pocket, then paused again and attached it to my little ring of picks and keys and such. As little good as the foot may have done its original rabbit owner, it had always been lucky for me, and nowadays I seemed to need all the help I could get. I took a last look around, wondering what I hoped to find. I picked up my telephone, wondered if it was tapped, decided that it probably wasn't. But who was I going to call? I hung up and found the phone book, which had received the dump and shake treatment like every other book in the apartment. I picked it up and looked for Elaine Christopher without success. There were several E. Christophers listed but none on Bank Street. I decided that the lady's listing or lack thereof was one of an ever-increasing number of things I couldn't be bothered to think about.

So I hefted my suitcase, killed the lights, opened the door, stepped out into the hallway, and there was Mrs. Hesch.

SHE was wearing a shapeless housedress with faded flowers on it. (Printed on it, that is. Not pinned to it or anything like that.) She had cloth slippers on her feet and her gray hair was pinned up in a sort of sloppy chignon. An unfiltered cigarette with a good half-inch of ash hung from the right corner of her wide mouth. I'd seen her in this outfit before, or in one very much like it. I'd also seen her dressed to the nines, but I'd never seen her without a cigarette smoldering in the corner of her mouth. She never took it out to talk and I'm not positive she removed it when she ate.

"Mr. Rhodenbarr," she said. "I thought I heard you moving around in there. Meaning I thought I heard somebody. I didn't know it was you."

"Uh," I said. "Well, it was."

"Yeah." Her bright little eyes took in the suitcase. "Going someplace? Not that I blame you. Poor boy, you got some kind of trouble for yourself, huh? The years we live across the hall from each other, you and me, and whoever would guess a nice boy like you would be a burglar? You never bothered anybody in this building, did you?"

"Of course not."

"Exactly what I said. You know the kind of conversations you hear in the laundry room. There are crazy women in this building, Mr. Rhodenbarr. One the other day, she's running off at the mouth like a broken record. 'We ain't safe in our own beds!' I said to her, 'Gert,' I said, 'in the first place you'd be safe in anybody's bed, believe me.' And I said to her, I said, 'When did Mr. Rhodenbarr ever hurt anybody? Who did he ever rob in this building, and who cares what he does over on the East Side, where the rich *momsers* deserve whatever happens to them?' You might as well be talking to a wall." Ashes spilled from her cigarette. "We shouldn't stand here like this," she said, her voice pitched lower. "Come on into my place, I got coffee on the stove."

"I'm really in sort of a rush, Mrs. Hesch."

"Don't be ridiculous. You always got time for a cup of my coffee. Since when are you in such a rush?"

I followed her into the apartment as if hypnotized. She poured me a cup of really excellent coffee and while I sipped it she stubbed out her cigarette and replaced it immediately with a fresh one. She went on to tell me how I'd brought no end of excitement to the building, how the police had been in and out of my apartment, and how there had been other visitors as well.

"I didn't see them," she said, "but the door was wide open when they left. It was yesterday afternoon when Jorge put the new lock on it. I saw what they did to your apartment. Like animals, Mr. Rhodenbarr. Except an animal wouldn't do nothing like that. Who was it? Cops?"

"I don't think so."

"You know who it was?"

"No, I wish I did. You didn't see them?"

"I don't even know when they were there. Such a mess they made you'd think I'd of heard them, but when I got the set going I don't hear nothing. You don't know who did this thing? Is it mixed up with the man you killed?"

"I never killed anybody, Mrs. Hesch."

She nodded thoughtfully, neither buying nor rejecting the statement. "I can imagine you a burglar," she said slowly. "But killing somebody is something else again. I said as much to the cop that questioned me."

"They questioned you?"

"They questioned the building, believe me. Listen, I didn't tell them a thing. I'll be honest with you, I got no use for the *momsers*. The time my niece Gloria was raped all they did was ask her stupid questions. What I told them about you was you're a nice boy who would never hurt a cockroach. I wouldn't tell a cop if his pants was on fire, believe me. But what he told me, the cop, he told me you ran into this Flaxford—that's his name?"

"Flaxford, right."

"He says when Flaxford discovered you, you panicked, but I thought about this, Mr. Rhodenbarr, and I don't know if I can see you killing somebody in a panic. You didn't do it?"

"Definitely not, Mrs. Hesch. In fact I'm trying to find out who did."

"If you say so." She was still keeping an open mind on the subject. "Though to be frank, those *momsers* on the East Side, what do I care if you did or didn't? They got it coming is how I look at it. This is good coffee, isn't it?"

"The best."

"Coffee's one thing I make a fuss about. You got to take the trouble or you're drinking dishwater. Maybe you're hungry, I didn't think to ask. You like cinnamon buns?"

"I just had breakfast, Mrs. Hesch, but thanks."

"Sit anyway. Where are you going? Sit, you'll have another cup. You don't have to be in such a hurry. One more cup of coffee ain't gonna kill you. Sit!"

I sat.

"So you're a burglar," she said. "You mind a personal question? You make a pretty decent living at it?"

"I manage."

She nodded. "Exactly what I told Whatsername in eleven-J. I said a bright boy like that, clean-cut and a good dresser, always a smile or a nice word for a person, I said if he ain't making a living he'll get into something else. But it's like talking to a wall, believe me, and then the other one, Gert, she starts in how she's not safe in her bed. The people in this building, Mr. Rhodenbarr, take it from me, it's like talking to a wall."

Chapter Twelve

MOST people who checked into the Cumberland had either a suitcase or a girl in tow. I was unusual in that I had one of each with me. My canvas suitcase looked slightly disreputable, but then so did my girl. She was wearing skintight jeans and a bright green sweater a size too small for her with no bra under it. And she'd done something moderately sluttish to her hair, and she was wearing dark lipstick and several pounds of eye shadow. She looked remarkably tawdry.

The clerk looked her over while I registered us as Mr. and Mrs. Ben G. Roper of Kansas City, which might have made more sense had my luggage been monogrammed. I gave him back the registration card along with a pair of ten-dollar bills, and while he was finding my change Ellie slid an envelope onto the counter. The clerk gave me $6.44 or thereabouts, then spotted the envelope with Brill's name printed on it and blinked. "Where'd this come from?" he wondered.

I shrugged and Ellie said she thought it was there all along. The clerk didn't seem terribly interested in this or much of anything else. He stuck it in a pigeonhole numbered 305.

Our own key was numbered 507. I grabbed my bag—there was no bellhop at the Cumberland—and Ellie walked with me to the elevator, her behind swaying professionally to and fro. The old man in the elevator cage chewed his cigar and took us up to the fifth floor without a word, then left us to let ourselves into our room.

It wasn't much of a room. The bed, which took up most of it, looked as though it had had hard use. Ellie sat lightly on the edge of it, removed makeup, did something to her hair to make it as it had been originally.

"A lot of trouble for nothing," she said.

"You enjoyed the masquerade."

"I suppose so. I still look like a tramp in this sweater."

"You certainly look like a mammal, I'll say that much."

She glowered at me. I checked my wig and cap in the bathroom mirror. They hadn't made much of an impression on Mrs. Hesch, who never even noticed that my hair had changed color.

"Let's go," I said, then did a Groucho Marx thing with my eyebrows. "Unless you'd like to make a couple of dollars, girlie."

"Here? Ugh."

"A bed is a bed is a bed."

"This one's no bed of roses. Do people actually have sex in rooms like this?"

"That's all they do. You don't think anyone would sleep here, do you?"

She wrinkled her nose and we left, taking our suitcase with us.

A call from Childs had established that Wesley Brill was out, and a knock on his door established that he hadn't come back yet. I could have picked his lock in a couple of seconds but it turned out that I didn't have to, because I stuck our room key in on a hunch and oddly enough it worked. Quite often the rooms on a particular line will respond to the same key—305 and 405 and 505, for instance—but now and then in older hotels the locks loosen up with age and a surprising number of keys turn out to be interchangeable.

Brill's room was nicer than the ones they used for the hot sheets trade. It still wasn't much but at least there was a piece of carpet covering some of the floor and the furniture was only on its penultimate legs. I put my suitcase on a chair, rummaged idly through Brill's closet and dresser, then took my suitcase off the chair, put it on the floor, and sat on the chair myself. There was another chair with arms, and Ellie had already taken it.

"Well," she said, "here we are."

"Here we are indeed."

"I wonder when he's coming back."

"Sooner or later."

"Good thinking. I don't suppose you thought to bring along a deck of cards?"

"I'm afraid not."

"That's what I thought."

"Well, I never thought of playing cards as proper equipment for a burglar."

"You always worked alone."

"Uh-huh. You'd think he'd have a deck of cards here. You'd think anyone who spent a lot of time in this room would play a lot of solitaire."

"And cheat."

"Most likely. I'd pace the floor if there was room. I find myself remembering bad stand-up comics. 'The room was so small . . .' "

"How small was it, Johnny?"

"The room was so small you had to go out in the hall to close the door."

"That small, eh?"

"The room was so small the mice were hunchbacked. I have to admit I've never understood that line. Why would mice be hunchbacked in a small room?"

"I think you've got an overly literal mind."

"I probably do."

She smiled. "You're nice, though. Just the same, literal mind or not, you're nice."

WE WOULD talk, fall silent, talk some more. At one point she asked me what I would do when it was all over.

"Go to jail," I said.

"Not once we find the real killer. They'll drop the other charges, won't they? I bet they will."

"They might."

"Well, what'll you do then? After it's all over?"

I thought about it. "Find a new apartment," I said at length. "I wouldn't be able to stay where I am, not even if those visitors hadn't turned it into a slum. All this publicity, the whole building knows about me. I'll have to move someplace else and take the apartment under another name. It'll be a nuisance but I guess I can live with it."

"You'll stay in New York?"

"Oh, I think so. I think I'd go crazy anywhere else. This is home. Besides, I'm connected here."

"How do you mean?"

"I know how to operate in New York. When I steal something I know who'll buy it and how to negotiate the sale. The cops know me, which in the long run does you more good than harm, although you might not think so. Oh, there's any number of reasons why a burglar is better off operating in territory that he knows in and out. I don't even like to work outside of Manhattan if I can avoid it. I remember one job I went on up in Harrison, that's in Westchester—"

"You're going to go on being a burglar."

I looked at her.

"I didn't realize that," she said. "You're going to keep on opening locks and stealing things?"

"What else?"

"I don't know."

"Ellie, on some level or other I think you think you're watching all of this on television and I'm going to reform right in time for the final commercial. That may keep the audience happy but it's not terribly realistic."

"It isn't?"

"Not really, no. I'm almost thirty-five years old. Opening locks and stealing things is the only trade I know. There's a lot of ads in *Popular Mechanics* telling me about career opportunities in meat-cutting and taxidermy but somehow I don't think they're being completely honest with me. And I don't figure I could cut it by raising chinchillas at home or growing ginseng in my backyard, and the only kind of work I'm qualified for pays two dollars an hour and would bore the ass off me before I'd earned ten dollars."

"You could be a locksmith."

"Oh, sure. They break their necks running around handing out licenses to convicted burglars. And the bonding companies are just standing in line to do business with locksmiths with criminal records."

"You must be qualified for something, Bernie."

"The state taught me how to make license plates and sew mailbags. This is going to stun you but there's very little call for either of those skills in civilian life."

"But you're intelligent, you're capable, you can think on your feet—"

"All important qualifications that help me make it as a burglar. Ellie, I've got a very good life. That's something you don't seem to realize. I work a couple of nights a year and I spend the rest of my time taking things easy. Is that such a bad deal?"

"No."

"I've been a burglar for years. Why should I change?"

"I don't know."

"Nobody changes."

WE DIDN'T have too much to say after that exchange. The time passed about as quickly as the Middle Ages. While we waited, the management kept renting out the room next door to us. Several times we heard footsteps in the hallway and sat motionless, thinking it might be Brill, and then the door next to us would open, and before long bedsprings would creak. Soon the bedsprings would cease creaking and shortly thereafter the footsteps would return to the elevator.

"True love," Ellie said.

"Well, it's nice the hotel serves a purpose."

"It does keep them off the streets. That last chap was in rather a hurry, wouldn't you say?"

"Probably had to get back to his office."

Then at last footsteps approached from the elevator but did not stop at the room next door. Instead they stopped directly in front of the door behind which we lurked. I drew a quick breath and got to my feet, padding soundlessly into position at the side of the door.

Then his key turned in the lock and the door opened and it was him all right, Wesley Brill, the man with the soft brown eyes that had never quite met mine, and I stood with my hands poised waist-high at my sides, ready to catch him if he fainted, ready to grab him if he tried to bolt, ready to hang a high hard one on his chin if he decided to get violent.

What he did was stare. "Rhodenbarr," he said. "This is utterly incredible. How on earth did you manage to find me? And they didn't tell me anyone was waiting for me."

"They didn't know it."

"But how did you—oh, of course. You're a burglar."

"Everybody's got to be something."

"Indeed."

His voice and his whole manner of speaking were completely different. The Runyonesque diction was gone and he no longer bit off his words at their final consonants. There was an archness to his inflections, a lilt that was either theatrical or slightly faggoty or both.

"Bernie Rhodenbarr," he said. Then he caught sight of Ellie, broadened his grin, raised a hand and lifted a brown trilby hat from his head. "Miss," he said, then turned his attention to me once more. "Just let me close this door," he said. "No need to share our business with a whole neighborhood of buyers and sellers. There. How on earth did you ever find me, if you don't mind my asking?"

"I saw you on television."

"Oh?"

"An old movie."

"And you recognized me?" He preened a bit. "Which film?"

"*The Man in the Middle.*"

"Not that dog with Jim Garner? I played a cabdriver in that one. I played a lot of cabdrivers." His eyes misted up at the memory. "No question about it, those were the days. Last year, God help us all, I *drove* a cab for a couple of weeks. Not in a film, but in what we call real life." He swung his arms back and forth, then put his little hands together and rubbed his palms as if to keep warm. "Those days are dead and gone. Let us live in the present, eh? The important thing is that she still wants the box."

I looked at him.

"That's why you looked me up, isn't it? The infamous blue leather box."

"Leather-covered," I said. Don't ask me why.

"Leather, leather-covered, whatever. Just so you've got it. As far as killing Flaxford, well, that certainly wasn't what she had in mind, but it's my impression she figures it couldn't have happened to a nicer guy. What she didn't know was whether you'd managed to pick up the box before you had to get out of there, but if you did she definitely wants it and she'll be glad to pay for it."

I stared at him, but of course his eyes didn't meet mine. They were aimed over my shoulder, as usual.

"Look, Bernie—" He grinned suddenly. "You don't mind if I

call you Bernie, do you? You know who I am and I don't have to play the heavy any longer, do I? And you can call me Wes."

"Wes," I said.

"Excellent. And I don't think I've met the little lady."

"C'mon, Wes. You're slipping back into character. Wesley Brill wouldn't say that. 'The little lady.' "

"You're absolutely right." He faced Ellie and made a rather courtly bow. "Wesley Brill," he said.

"Ruth Hightower," I said.

He smiled. "Not really."

"That's a private joke," Ellie said. "I'm Ellie Christopher, Wes."

"My pleasure, Miss Christopher."

She said he could call her Ellie, and he told her to call him Wes, which she'd already done, and he added that no one called him Wesley, that indeed his name had originally been John Wesley Brill, his mother having seen fit to name him for the founder of Methodism, a move she might not have dared had she suspected he was destined for an actor's life. He'd dropped his first name entirely the first time he trod the boards. (That was his phrase, trod the boards.) Ellie assured him that she thought dropping a first name altogether was perfectly all right but that when you retained an initial out in front it was a sign of a devious character. Good ol' Wes said he couldn't agree more. Ellie mentioned G. Gordon Liddy and E. Howard Hunt and Wes chimed in with J. Edgar Hoover. While they were at it I thought of F. Scott Fitzgerald and decided there might be a few weak spots in Ellie's theory.

"Wes," I cut in, "the purpose of our call wasn't entirely social."

"I'd guess not. You're up to your neck in it, aren't you? Killing old J. Francis. That really surprised her because she said you never impressed her as violent. I told her it must have been self-defense. Although I don't suppose the law calls it self-defense when it happens in the middle of a burglary."

"The law calls it first-degree murder."

"I know. It doesn't seem entirely fair, does it? But the big question, Bernie, is, have you got the box?"

"The box."

"Right."

I closed my eyes for a minute. "You never actually saw the box yourself," I said. "Because you described it very precisely but you didn't know what color blue it was. And you didn't make up an answer when I asked."

"Why would I make up an answer?"

"You'd make one up if there was no box in the first place. But there really is a box, isn't there?"

He peered intently at me and his forehead developed a single vertical line just above the nose like the one David Janssen has in the Excedrin commercial, the one that makes you certain he really does have one rat bastard of a headache.

"The box exists," I said.

"You mean you thought—"

"That's what I thought."

"Which means you don't—"

"Right. I don't."

"Shit," he said, pronouncing the word as emphatically as if he'd just stepped in it. Then he remembered that the little lady was present. "I beg your pardon," he said.

She told him not to worry about it.

THERE REALLY WAS A BOX. In fact he'd been waiting for me in Pandora's that first night, sitting in a back booth with four thousand dollars on his hip, stretching out his drinks until they closed the place. It wasn't until the following day that he found out what had gone wrong.

"And you didn't kill Flaxford," he said, after I'd done some recapping on my own.

"And neither did you."

"Me? Kill the man? I never even met him. Oh, I see what you mean. You thought I set you up. But if *you* didn't kill Flaxford—"

"Somebody else did. Because beating your own head in with a blunt instrument is no way to commit suicide."

"I wish I knew more about this," he said. "I'm not really in the center of things. There's a lot happening I don't know about."

"I know how you feel."

"All I am is an actor, really. And that career's not going too well. One thing leads to another, and I had this drinking situation that's over with now, thank God, but I reached a point where I couldn't remember lines. I still have trouble. I can improvise, which is what I was doing the two times I saw you, building a role around a framework, but you can't do that in the movies unless you're directed by Robert Altman or something. The jobs stopped coming, and this agent I'm with now, I'd have to say he's more pimp than agent."

"I know. I was in his office."

"You met Pete?"

"I was in his office," I repeated, "but he wasn't. Last night. To get your address."

"Oh," he said. He looked for a moment at his own door, no doubt reflecting on its failure to keep us out of his room. "The point is, I'm in this because I'm an actor. I used to play a lot of heavies and that's what she hired me for, to hire you to get the box and then to pay you off and take the box to her."

"How did you know to hire me?"

"She told me to."

"Right, sure," I said. "She told you to hire a burglar. But how did you happen to know that I happened to be one?"

He frowned. "She told me to hire you," he said. "You specifically, Bernard Rhodenbarr. I'm an *actor*, Bernie. How would I go about finding a burglar on my own? I don't know any burglars. I can *play* crooks but that doesn't mean I hang around with them."

"Oh."

"I used to know a bookie but since off-track betting came in I couldn't tell you if he's alive or dead. As far as burglars are concerned, well, I now know one burglar, or—" with a nod to Ellie "—or possibly two, but that's all."

"The woman who hired you," Ellie said. "She knew Bernie was a burglar."

"That's right."

"And she knew where he lived and what he looked like, is that right?"

"Well, she took me over there and pointed him out to me."

"How did she know him?"

"Search me."

Loren the cop would have frisked him. I just said, "What's her name, Wes?"

"I'm supposed to keep her name out of this."

"I'm sure you are."

"That's why she hired me in the first place."

Ellie's eyes flashed. "Now you just wait a damned minute," she said. "Don't you think Bernie has a right to know who got him into this mess? He's wanted for a murder he didn't commit and he's taking a chance every time he sets foot outside, and he has to go around wearing a disguise—"

"The hair," Wes said. "I knew something was different. You dyed your hair."

"It's a wig.

"Really? It looks remarkably natural."

"God *damn* it," Ellie said. "How can you have the nerve to tell us the woman doesn't want her name mentioned?"

"Well, she doesn't."

"Well, that's too bad. You'll just have to tell us who she is or else."

"Or else what?" he asked. Reasonably, I thought.

Ellie frowned, then glanced at me for help. But I was getting flashes and the tumblers were beginning to drop. Brill hadn't known me, hadn't even known I was a burglar. But this woman had hired him to rope me in, selecting him because he was an actor who had made a career out of playing underworld types. She didn't know any real underworld types, nor did she know any real burglars except for me, but she did know who I was and where I lived and what I looked like and how I kept the wolf away from my door.

I said, "Wait a minute."

"You can't let him get away with it, Bernie."

"Just hold it for a minute."

"You can't. We found him and we trapped him and now he's supposed to tell us what we want to know. Isn't that the way it's supposed to go?"

I closed my eyes and said, "Cool it, will you? Just for a minute."

And the last tumbler tumbled and the mental lock eased open so sweetly, so gently, like the petals of a flower, like a yielding lady. I opened my eyes and beamed at Ellie, then turned the warmth of my smile on Wesley Brill.

"He doesn't have to tell me a thing," I said to Ellie. "It's enough that he told me it was a woman. That triggered it, really. A woman who doesn't know anything about crime except that a guy named Bernie Rhodenbarr burgles for a living. I know who she is."

"Who?"

"Does she still live in the same place, Wes? Park Avenue, right? I don't remember the address offhand but I could draw you a floor plan of the apartment. I tend to remember the layout of places where I've been arrested."

Brill was perspiring. Beads of sweat dotted his forehead and he wiped them away not with his whole hand but with an extended index finger. The gesture was very familiar. I must have seen him do it dozens of times in movies.

"Mrs. Carter Sandoval," I said. "Didn't I tell you about the Sandovals, Ellie? Of course I did. Her husband had a monster coin collection that I'd taken an interest in. He also had a monster of a gun and his doorbell was out of order and he and his wife were home when I came a-calling. I'm sure I told you about this."

"Yes, you did."

"I thought so." I grinned at Brill. "Her husband was head of CACA. That's not a bathroom word, it stands for the Civic Anti-Crime Association or something like that. It's a group of high-minded pests who push for everything from more foot patrolmen on the beat to investigations of political and judicial corruption.

The sonofabitch held a gun on me and I tried to buy my way out, and he was the wrong man to offer a bribe to. He even wanted to prosecute me for attempted bribery but he wasn't a cop, for God's sake, and there's no law against trying to bribe a private citizen. At least I don't think there is, but come to think of it I'm probably wrong. There's a law against just about everything, isn't there? Of course I didn't know he was the head CACA person. All I knew was that he did something terribly profitable on Wall Street and thought rare coins were a hell of a hedge against inflation. Does he still have the coins, Wes?"

Brill just stared at me.

"I remember them well," I said. I was enjoying this. "And they would remember me, Wes. I saw them the night I was arrested, of course, but they were also on hand when I went before the judge. They didn't have to be. I copped a plea to a lesser charge, and don't think that didn't take some doing. Carter Sandoval wasn't nuts about the idea of that. But somebody must have taken him aside and explained that the courts would never get anything done if every criminal went through the ritual of a jury trial, and he must have decided it would get more of us evildoers off the streets if the system was allowed to go along as usual, so he and his wife showed up to watch me stand up and plead guilty and get sent away to the license plate factory. I suppose he figured it would be good publicity for his cause with him there to watch justice triumph. And I think he got a personal kick out of it, too. He seemed pretty attached to those coins and thoroughly steamed at the thought of me violating the sanctity of his home."

"Bernie—"

"She was a lot younger than him. She must have been around forty or close to it, so I guess she's around forty-five now.

Good-looking woman. A little too much jawline for my taste, but maybe she was just setting her jaw with determination the times I saw her. Is her hair still the same color, Wes?"

"I never told you her name."

"That's true, Wes, and I wish you would. It's on the tip of my tongue. It's not Carla and it's not Marla and what the hell is it?"

"Darla."

Something made me glance at Ellie. Her shoulders were set and her head cocked forward. She looked to be concentrating intently. "Darla Sandoval," I said. "Right. That ring any kind of a bell for you, Ellie?"

"No. I don't think you mentioned her name before. Why?"

"No reason. Why don't you call her, Wes?"

"She calls me. I'm not supposed to call her."

"Call her and see if she wants the box back."

"But you don't *have* the box, Bernie." He eyed me in his oblique fashion. "Or do you? I'm getting more confused by the minute. Do you have the box or don't you?

"I don't."

"I didn't think so because you didn't even believe there *was* a box. You didn't get the box from Flaxford's apartment, then. Did you see it there and—"

"No."

"You went through the desk? There was a desk there, wasn't there? A large rolltop?"

"There was, and I went through it pretty carefully. But I couldn't find any kind of blue box in it."

"Shit," he said, and this time he didn't think to apologize to Ellie. I don't think she minded. I'm not even sure she heard him. She seemed to have something else on her mind.

"That means they got it," he said.

"Who?"

"Whoever killed him. You didn't commit the murder or steal the box, so somebody else did both those little things and that's why the box was gone when you got there. So that's the end of everything."

"Call Darla."

"What's the point?"

"I know where the box is," I said. "Call her."

Chapter Thirteen

HER hair was still blond, and if she had changed much in any other respect I didn't notice it. She was still slim and elegant, with strength in her face and assurance in her carriage. Wes and I met her as arranged over the phone at a brownstone apartment a few blocks from the one I'd been caught burgling a few years back. She opened the door, greeted me by name, and told Wes his presence would not be necessary.

"You run along, Wesley. It's quite all right, Mr. Rhodenbarr and I will work things out." It was the dismissal of a servant, and whether he liked it or not he took it without a murmur. She was swinging the door shut even as he was turning. She bolted it—with the burglar already inside, I thought—and favored me with a cool and regal smile. She asked if I'd like a drink and I said Scotch would be fine and told her how to fix it.

While she made the drinks I stood around thinking of Ellie. She'd decided rather abruptly that she wouldn't come along to

meet Darla Sandoval. A quick glance at her watch, a sudden real-
ization that it was much later than she'd thought, an uncertain bit
of chatter about an unspecified appointment for which she was
already late, a promise to meet me back at Rodney's apartment
later on, and away she went. I'd see her later, after her appointment had been kept, after her legendary cats had been fed, after
her legendary stained-glass sculpture had been assembled . . .

I was running various thoughts through my mind when Darla
Sandoval came back with drinks for both of us. Hers was a darker
shade of amber than mine. She raised her glass as if to toast, failed
to hit on a suitable phrase, and looked slightly less than certain
for the first time in our acquaintance. "Well," she said, which was
toast enough, and we took sips of our drinks. It was excellent
Scotch and this did not much surprise me.

"Nice place you've got here."

"Oh, this? I borrowed it from a friend."

"Still live at the same spot? Where we met?"

"Oh, yes. Nothing's changed." She sighed. "I want you to
know I'm sorry about all this," she said, sounding apologetic if
not devastated. "I never expected to get you involved in anything
so complicated. I thought you'd do a very simple job of burglary
for me. I remembered how skillfully you opened our locks that
night—"

"That was skill, all right. Hitting the place with you two in it."

"Accidents do happen. I thought you'd do perfectly, though,
and of course you're the only person I know who could possibly
do the job. I remembered you, of course, your name, and I just
glanced through the telephone book on the chance that you
might be in it, and there you were."

"There I was," I agreed. "They charge extra for an unlisted

number and I've always considered it a waste of money. The idea of paying them for an unperformed service. Goes against the grain."

"I never thought Fran would be home that night. There was an opening downtown."

"An opening?"

"An experimental play. He was supposed to be in the audience and at the cast party afterward. Carter and I were there, you see, and when Fran didn't turn up I got very nervous. I knew you were going to be burgling his apartment and I didn't know where he could be, whether he'd gone somewhere else or stayed home or what. Wesley says you didn't kill him."

"He was dead when I got there."

"And the police—"

I gave her a quick summary of what had happened in Flaxford's apartment. Her eyes widened when I mentioned how I'd arranged to buy my way out. Here her husband was battling police corruption and she didn't seem to know that cops took money from crooks. I guess civilians just don't understand how the system works.

"Then someone else actually killed him," she said. "I don't suppose it could have been accidental? No, of course it couldn't. But you did look in the desk before the police came? I saw Fran put the box in the desk. It was a deep blue, a little darker than royal blue, and the box itself was about the size of a hardcover novel. Maybe larger, perhaps as big as a dictionary. And I saw him put it in the desk."

"Where in the desk? Under the rolltop?"

"One of the lower drawers. I don't know which one."

"It doesn't matter. I went through those drawers."

"Thoroughly?"

"Very thoroughly. If the box was there I would have found it."

"Then someone else got it first." Her face paled slightly beneath her makeup. She drank some more of her drink, sat down in a straight chair with a needlepoint seat. "Whoever killed Fran took the box," she said.

"I don't think so. That desk was locked when I found it, Mrs. Sandoval. Desk locks are always easy to open but you have to know what you're doing."

"The killer could have had a key."

"But would he have bothered to lock up afterward? With a corpse in the bedroom? I don't think so. He'd have thrown things all over the place and left a mess behind him." I thought of my own ravaged apartment. "Besides," I went on, "somebody's still looking for the box and you don't go on looking for something you already have. I went back to my own place a couple of hours ago and it looked as though Attila had marched his Huns through it. You didn't have anything to do with that, did you?"

"Of course not."

"Well, you could have hired someone. No hard feelings if you did, but you'd better tell me or we'll be wasting our time chasing wild geese."

She assured me she had had nothing to do with looting my place and I decided she was telling the truth. I hadn't really figured she'd been involved in the first place. It was more logical to assume it had been tossed by the same person who had scrambled Flaxford's brains.

"I think I know where the box is," I said.

"Where?"

"Where it's been all along. Flaxford's apartment."

"You said you looked."

"I looked in the desk, but that's as far as I got. I'd have kept on looking if the Marines hadn't landed and I think I probably would have found it. It could have been anywhere in the apartment. Just because you saw him put it in the desk doesn't mean he left it there forever. Maybe he had a wall safe behind a picture. Maybe he stuck it in a drawer in the bedside table. It could even be in the desk but not in a drawer. Those old rolltops have secret compartments. Maybe he put the box in one of them after you left. Anyway, I'll bet it's still there, right where he put it, and the killer assumes I've got it, and the apartment's all locked up with a police seal on the door."

"What can we do?"

An idea began heating up in the back of my mind. I let it simmer there while I took a different tack with her. "This blue box," I said. "I think it's time I knew what was inside it."

"Is it important?"

"It's important to you and it's important to the man who killed Flaxford. That makes it important to me. Whatever it is must be pretty valuable."

"Only to me."

"He was blackmailing you."

A nod.

"Photographs? Something like that?"

"Photographs, tape recordings. He showed me some pictures and played part of a tape for me." She shuddered. "I knew he didn't love me any more than I loved him. But I thought he enjoyed what we did." She stood up, took a few steps toward the window. "My life with my husband is quite conventional, Mr. Rhodenbarr. Some years ago I learned that I'm not all that conventional myself. When I met Fran some months ago we learned we had certain, uh, tastes in common." She turned to face me. "I never expected to be blackmailed."

"What did he want from you? Money?"

"No. I don't have any money. I had a hard time raising enough cash to hire you and Wesley. No, Fran wanted me to influence my husband. You know he's involved with CACA."

"I know."

"There's a man named Michael Debus. He's the District Attorney of Brooklyn or Queens, I can never remember which. Carter's spearheading some sort of investigation which threatens to expose this Debus."

"And Flaxford wanted you to pull the plug on it?"

"Yes. As if I could, incorruptible as Carter is."

"What was Flaxford's interest?"

"I don't know. I can't figure out how he fits into it all. He and I became involved long before Carter began this investigation, so he didn't start seeing me with an ulterior motive in mind. And I always understood that he was involved with the theater. He produced some shows off-off-Broadway, you know, and he moved in those circles. That's how I met him."

"And that's how you met Brill also?"

"Yes. He didn't know Fran or any of my other theater friends, which made me feel safer about using him. But Fran must have been involved with crime in some way that I never knew about."

"He must have been some kind of a fixer," I said. "He was obviously trying to fix things for Debus."

"Well, he certainly fixed me." She came over, sat down on a love seat, took a cigarette from a box on the coffee table, lit it with a butane table lighter. "He must have known just what he was doing when he started up with me," she said levelly. "Even if the Debus investigation hadn't started. He knew who Carter was and he must have decided that it would come in handy sooner or later to have a hold on me."

"Did your husband ever meet him?"

"Two or three times when I dragged Carter to an opening or a party. I'm interested in the theater the way Carter is interested in collecting coins. With those small companies you can have the excitement of being a backer and the thrill of being an insider for a couple of hundred deductible dollars. It's an inexpensive way to delude yourself into thinking you're involved in creative work with creative people. Oh, you meet the most interesting people that way, Mr. Rhodenbarr."

She took our empty glasses into the kitchen. I think she may have helped herself to a slug from the bottle while she was at it because when she came back her face had softened and she seemed more at ease.

I asked her when Flaxford had shown her the contents of the blue box.

"About two weeks ago. It was only the fourth time I'd been to his apartment. We generally came here. This isn't a friend's apartment, you see. I rented it myself some years ago as a convenience."

"I'm sure it's convenient."

"It is." She drew on her cigarette. "Of course he took me to his apartment so he could make the tapes and photographs. And then he invited me up to show me his work and make his pitch."

"He told you to get your husband to drop the Debus investigation?"

"Yes."

"But you couldn't do that?"

"Tell Carter to discontinue a CACA project?" She laughed. "You ought to remember just how high-principled a man my husband is, Mr. Rhodenbarr. You tried to bribe him, remember?"

"I do indeed. Didn't you say as much to Flaxford?"

"Of course I did. He said he was just trying to give me a chance to work things out on my own. For the sake of our friendship, he said." She gritted her teeth. "But if I couldn't sway Carter myself, then he'd go to him directly, threaten to circulate the photos."

"What would Carter have done?"

"I don't know. I'm not certain. He couldn't have allowed the photographs to circulate. Carter Sandoval's wife doing perverted things? No, he could hardly have tolerated that, no more than he could have tolerated remaining married to me. I'm not sure just what he would have done. He might have tried something dramatic, something like leaving a detailed note implicating Fran and Debus and then diving out a window."

"Would he have tried killing Flaxford?"

"Carter? Commit murder?"

"He might not have thought of it as murder."

Her eyes narrowed. "I can't imagine him doing it," she said. "Anyway, he was with me at the theater."

"The whole night?"

"We had dinner together and then we drove downtown."

"And you were together the entire time?"

She hesitated. "There was a one-act curtain raiser before the main production. An experimental extended scene written by Gulliver Shane. I don't know if you're familiar with his work."

"I'm not. Is Carter?"

"Pardon?"

"He missed the curtain-raiser, didn't he?"

She nodded. "He dropped me in front of the theater and then went to park the car. The curtain was at eight thirty and I had time for a cigarette in the lobby so he must have dropped me at twenty after eight. Then he had trouble finding a parking place. He won't park by a hydrant even though they don't tow cars away that far downtown. He's so disgustingly honest."

"So he missed the curtain."

"If you're not seated when the lights go up you have to watch from the back of the theater. So he couldn't sit next to me during the Shane play. But he said he watched from the back, and he was sitting beside me by nine o'clock, or maybe nine fifteen at the outside. That wouldn't have given him enough time to rush all the way uptown and kill Fran and get back to me that quickly, would it?"

I didn't say anything.

"And Carter wouldn't even have known about Fran. Fran hadn't gone to him yet, I know he hadn't. I was supposed to have until the end of the week. And Carter wouldn't kill anyone by striking him. He'd use a gun."

"Does he still have that cannon of his?"

"Yes. It's a horrible thing, isn't it?"

"You don't know the half of it. You didn't have it pointed at you. But suppose Carter didn't plan any murder. Suppose Flaxford confronted him with the photos and he reacted on the spur of the moment. He wouldn't have had the gun with him, and—"

I left it right there because it didn't make any sense. It wasn't just that Sandoval would have been acting completely out of character. Beyond that, there was no reason for Flaxford to have met him at that hour or to have been wearing a dressing gown during the confrontation. And if a man like Carter Sandoval did kill anyone in a blind rage, which was hard enough to believe, he certainly would have given himself up and taken his punishment afterward.

"Forget all that," I said. "Carter didn't do it."

"I didn't see how he could have."

"It keeps coming back to the blue box," I told her. "We have to get our hands on it. You want those photos and tapes before some opportunist gets his hands on them. And I want to find out what's in the box besides tapes and pictures."

"You think there's something else?"

"I think there has to be. You and your husband are the only people who'd be interested in the tapes and pictures. But if neither of you killed Flaxford and neither of you sacked my apartment, then there has to be something else for somebody else to be looking for. And once we know what it is we'll have a shot at knowing who's looking for it."

She started to say something but I tuned her out. An idea was beginning to glimmer. I picked up my glass, then put it down without drinking anything. No more liquor tonight, not for Bernard. He had work to do.

"Money," I said.

"In the blue box?"

"That's always possible, I suppose. But that's not what I'm talking about. You were going to pay me another four thousand dollars. Have you still got it?"

"Yes."

"At home?"

"Here, as a matter of fact. Why?"

"Can you raise any more?"

"Maybe two or three thousand over the next few days."

"No time for that. Your four thousand and my five thousand is nine thousand—isn't it impressive the way I can work out these sums in my head—nine thousand might be enough. Ten thousand would be a lot better. Could you dig up an extra thousand dollars in the next couple of hours if you put your mind to it?"

"I suppose I could. I'm thinking who I could ask. Yes, I could manage a thousand dollars. Why?"

I opened my suitcase, took out the three books. I gave Gibbon to Darla Sandoval and kept Barbara Tuchman and beekeeping for myself. "Every thirty pages or so," I said, talking as I riffled pages, "you will find two pages glued together. Tear them open—" I suited action to words "—and you'll find a hundred-dollar bill."

"Where did you get these books?"

"Mostly on Fourth Avenue. Not *Guns of August*, that came from Book-of-the-Month Club. Oh, you thought I stole them. No, this is my stash, my case money. I may have stolen the money but the books are all my own. They've been shaken and riffled and all, but they've refused to give up their secret. Come on, now. If we both work we'll get the money that much faster."

"But what are we going to do with it?"

"We are going to put your five thousand and my five thousand together," I said, "and that will give us ten thousand dollars, and we're going to use it to get me into J. Francis Flaxford's apartment, past the doorman and through the police evidence seal and everything. We're going to do it in the most expedient way possible. We're going to hire a police escort."

Chapter Fourteen

I SAT back in my chair and watched Ray Kirschmann count hundred-dollar bills. He performed his operation in silence but he did move his lips as he counted so it was easy for me to keep up with him. When he was all done he said, "Ten thousand, all right. That's what you said."

"Ten thousand two hundred, Ray. I must have had some bills stuck together. Careless of me. Leave two of them on the table there, huh? The price we set was ten even."

"Jesus," he said, but he put a pair of hundreds on the glass-topped coffee table before shuffling the remaining ten thou into a neat if bulky roll. "This is crazy," he said. "Dizziest damn thing I ever did. Dizziest damn thing I ever heard of, to tell you the truth."

"It's also the easiest money you ever made in your life."

"I'm takin' a hell of a risk, Bernie."

"What risk? You've got every right in the world to want to

have another look at the Flaxford apartment, you and Loren. You were the two cops who caught the original squeal and you were right in the middle of everything."

"Don't remind me."

"So there's something you have a feeling you may have missed, so you pick up the keys and get a warrant or permission slip or whatever the hell you get, and you and Loren go let yourselves into Flaxford's place."

"Except it ain't Loren."

"So instead of one skinny guy in a blue uniform you have a different skinny guy in a blue uniform. All cops look alike, you know that."

"Jesus."

"If you want to put the money back on the table—"

He gave me a sour look. I was in the same apartment where I'd met Darla Sandoval but I was drinking instant Yuban now instead of Scotch, and Darla herself was tucked away behind a pair of louvered doors in the kitchen. Since half of the ten grand was hers I figured she had every right in the world to listen in on our arrangements, but I also figured she'd be better off not meeting Ray Kirschmann face to face. If he'd even bothered to wonder whose apartment we were using he'd kept his curiosity to himself. Outside of a conventional *Nice place you got here, Rhodenbarr* we might as well have been meeting over hot dogs at Nedick's.

"I just don't know," he said now. "A fugitive from justice, an escaped murderer—"

"Ray, all I ever killed is time. I already told you that."

"Yeah."

"You don't honestly think I killed Flaxford, do you?"

"I got no opinion on the subject, Bernie. You're the same

fugitive from a homicide charge whether you killed him or he died of an ingrown toenail." He frowned at an irksome memory. "If you *didn't* do it," he said, "why in the hell did you jump me the way you did? Made me feel like seven different kinds of an asshole."

"I was stupid, Ray. I got spooked."

"Yeah, spooked."

"If I'd already known Flaxford was dead on the floor I wouldn't have gone nuts like that, but it shocked me, same as it shocked Loren, and I—"

"When Loren gets shocked he faints. It's a lot less hostile, just closing your eyes and hitting the rug."

"Next time I'll faint."

"Yeah."

"I'm going to find something in that apartment that'll point straight at the real killer. Because I *know* I didn't kill anybody, Ray, and I'll find out who did, and when I've got it worked out I'll hand it to you and look what a hero you'll be. 'The resourceful cop who dug beneath the surface to get at the real truth.' You're a safe bet to make plainclothes on the strength of that."

"Yeah, plainclothes. When you tell it I come out of it with a promotion. When I work it out on my own I see myself winding up stepping on my cock."

"Forget that, Ray. A promotion and ten grand, that's how you'll wind up."

"Don't forget I got to split with Loren." I shot him a doubtful look and he gave me back an injured expression in exchange. "Right down the middle," he said. "It's the same fuckin' risk for the both of us. You'll be wearin' his badge and twirlin' his nightstick, for Chrissake. Be his gun on your hip. If the shit hits the fan he'll be right there in front of it, arm in arm with me. So it's five grand for him and five grand for me."

"Sounds fair to me."

He looked at me for a moment, then let out air in a soundless whistle. He patted the bulky package on the sofa beside him. "Size thirty-eight long," he said. "That's what you ordered, right?"

"That's what I take."

"Loren's smaller'n you so I picked this up new. Maybe you better try it on."

I unwrapped the parcel, got out of my own clothes, donned a pair of regulation police blues over a blue shirt. There was no cap; I would wear Loren's. When I was dressed Ray inspected me, tugged here and there on the uniform, frowned, stepped back, shrugged, shook his head doubtfully and turned aside.

"I don't know," he said. "You don't look like New York's Finest to me."

"Just so I'm not a disgrace to the uniform."

"I guess it ain't too bad of a fit. It don't look tailor-made, you got to admit that, but then you also got to admit that neither does Loren's."

I took a moment to picture Loren. "No," I agreed, "he doesn't look as though the uniform was stitched together around him." I patted my trousers, pressed out imaginary wrinkles. "So I guess I'll do," I said.

"Yeah," he said. "I guess you'll do."

I was still in uniform when he left. After the door closed behind him Darla Sandoval emerged from the kitchen. She looked me up and down and raised her eyebrows.

"Well?"

"I think you look like a policeman. There's a mirror on the bedroom door if you want to see yourself."

I wouldn't have been surprised if there had been a mirror on the bedroom ceiling. (Well, maybe I would have.) But I went and checked my reflection on the mirrored door and decided I cut a reasonably dashing figure. I returned to the living room and agreed with Darla that I looked like a cop.

"He took all our money," she said. "Do you think that was wise?"

"I think it was inevitable. You can't pay cops half in advance and the balance upon delivery. You ought to be able to but they don't like to work that way."

"He's picking you up here tonight."

I nodded. "At twenty-one hundred hours. That's nine o'clock in English but he said it in cop talk because I was wearing the uniform."

"So you'll just wait for him here?"

I shook my head. "I'll go back to where I'm staying downtown. I didn't want to complicate things by having him meet me there. I'd just as soon he didn't know where I'm staying."

"Suppose he doesn't show up, Bernard? Then what?"

"He'll show. He'll even make sure he's on time because he doesn't want anything to go wrong. He'll bring Loren and I'll equip myself with all of Loren's paraphernalia, the badge and the cap and the gun and the nightstick and the cuffs, all that crap, and Loren'll curl up here with an astrology magazine while Ray and I go and do the dirty deed. Then Ray'll drop me back here and pick up Loren and that's the end of it."

"But suppose he keeps the ten thousand dollars and forgets all about you?"

"Oh," I said, "he won't do that."

"How can you be sure?"

"He's honest," I said, and when she stared at me I explained. "There's all kinds of honest. If a cop like Ray makes a deal he'll stick with it. He's that kind of honest. And you heard him carry on when I showed some doubt about his giving Loren an even split. He was genuinely offended at the implication. What's so funny?"

"I was thinking of Carter. He wouldn't understand a syllable of this."

"Well, he's a different kind of honest."

"He certainly is. Bernard, I think I can have one more drink without harming myself any. Can I get you one?"

"No thanks."

"You're sure?"

"Positive."

"More coffee, then?"

I shook my head. She went back to the kitchen and returned with drink in hand. She sat down on the sofa, sipped her drink, set it down on the coffee table and noticed the pair of hundred-dollar bills I'd convinced Ray to leave behind. "I guess these are yours," she said.

"Well, one of us counted wrong, Mrs. Sandoval."

"Darla."

"Darla. Why don't we each take one of them?"

That struck her as fair. She kept a bill and passed its brother to me. Then she said, "You said he was honest. That policeman. But he would have kept the extra two hundred dollars."

"Oh, sure. He was steamed when I called him on it."

"There really are all kinds of honesty, aren't there?"

"There really are."

It was time to change back into mufti, time to pack up the uniform and cart it downtown. But for the moment I didn't feel much like moving. I sat in a chair across from Darla and watched her nibble at her drink.

"Bernard? I was thinking that it's a waste of time for you to chase downtown and back. And it's an added risk, isn't it? Being out on the street that much?"

"I'll take cabs both ways."

"Even so."

"A small risk, I suppose."

"You could stay here, you know."

"I'd like to drop my suitcase at the place where I'm staying."

"Oh?"

"And there's someone I'll want to see before I meet Ray this evening. And a stop or two I'll want to make."

"I see."

Our eyes met. She had a lot of presence, this lady did. And something more than that.

"You really look effective in that uniform," she said.

"Effective?"

"Very effective. I'm just sorry I won't be able to be here tonight when you have all the accessories. The nightstick and the handcuffs and the badge and the gun."

"Well, you can imagine how I'll look with the props."

"Yes, I certainly can." She ran the tip of her tongue very purposefully over her lips. "Costumes can be very useful, you know. I sometimes think that's what I like most about theater. Not that the actors wear costumes physically, although they often do, but that the whole character which an actor puts on is a sort of costume."

"Do you do any acting yourself, Darla?"

"Oh, no, I'm just a dabbler. I told you that, didn't I? Why should you think I might have acted?"

"The way you were using your voice just then."

She licked her lips again. "Costumes," she said, and ran her eyes over my uniform. "I think I told you that I used to consider myself a very conventional person."

"I think you did."

"Yes, I'm quite sure I said that."

"Yes."

"Conventional in sexual matters."

"Yes."

"But in recent years I've found out otherwise. I may have told you that."

"Uh, yes, I think you did."

"In fact I'm positive I did."

"Yes."

She got to her feet and stood in such a way as to make me very much aware of the shape of her body. "If you were to wear that uniform," she said, "or one rather like it, and if you were to have handcuffs and a nightstick, I think I would find you quite irresistible."

"Uh."

"And we might do the most extraordinary things. Imaginative persons could probably find interesting things to do with handcuffs and a nightstick."

"Probably."

"And with each other."

"Very probably."

"Of course you might be too conventional for that sort of thing."

176

"I'm not all that conventional."

"No, I didn't really think you were. Do you find me attractive?"

"Yes."

"I hope you're not saying that out of politeness."

"I'm not."

"That's good. I'm older than you, of course. That wouldn't bother you?"

"Why should it?"

"I've no idea. It wouldn't?"

"No."

She nodded thoughtfully. "This is not the right time for us," she said.

"And I don't have the cuffs or the stick."

"No, you don't. But as an experiment, why don't you come kiss me?"

It was a stirring kiss. We were standing, her arms around my neck, and midway through the kiss I dropped my hands to her buttocks and took hold of them and squeezed with all my strength, whereupon she made some extraordinary sounds and quivered a bit. Eventually we let go of each other and she stepped backward.

"After all of this is over, Bernard—"

"Yes. Definitely."

"The uniform wouldn't even be all that important. Or the other paraphernalia."

"No, but it might be fun."

"Oh, it would definitely be fun." She licked her lips again. "I want to wash up. And you'll want to change, or do you plan to wear the uniform downtown?"

"No, I'll change."

I was in my own clothes by the time she returned from the bathroom, the heat flush gone from her face, the lipstick replenished on her mouth. I put on my silly yellow wig and fixed my cap in place over it. She gave me keys for the front door and the door to the apartment so that I would be able to let myself in when I returned. I didn't remind her that I could manage without them.

She said, "Bernard? That two hundred dollars the policeman was going to keep?"

"What about it?"

"Would he have divided it with his partner?"

I had to think about it, and finally I told her I just didn't know.

She smiled. "It's a good question, isn't it?"

"Yes," I said. "It's a very good question."

I GOT back to Rod's place before Ellie did. While I waited for her I tried my cop suit on again and frowned at my shoes. Did cops wear scotch-grain loafers? It seemed to me that they always wore square-toed black oxfords, occasionally switching to black wing tips. But did they ever wear loafers?

I decided it didn't matter. Nobody was going to be staring at my feet.

When Ellie walked in my outfit gave her a giggling fit. This didn't do wonders for my self-confidence. "But you can't be a cop," she said. "You're a crook!"

"The two aren't mutually exclusive."

"You just don't look like a cop, Bernie."

"Cops don't look like cops anymore," I pointed out. "Oh, older bulls like Ray still look the part, but the younger generation's gone to hell. Ray's partner's a good example. Bumping his nightstick into his knee, asking me what my sign was, then collapsing in a dead faint. I look as much like a cop as he does. Anyway, the only person I have to convince is a doorman. And I'll be with Ray and he'll do all the talking."

"I guess," she said.

"Don't you think it's a good idea?"

"I suppose so. You really think it's still there? The blue box?"

"If it was there in the first place it's there now. I think I know who turned my apartment inside out. I think it was a couple of people from Michael Debus's office." Probably the two men I'd seen going into my building two nights ago, I thought. While I'd stood on the corner looking up at my lighted windows they'd been busy turning order into chaos. "He's a D.A. in Brooklyn or Queens and he was connected to Flaxford."

"Flaxford was blackmailing him, too?"

"I don't think so, I think he was Debus's fixer. Carter Sandoval was making things hot for Debus, and Flaxford was putting pressure on Mrs. Sandoval to call her husband off. Debus must have been worried that something incriminating was left on the premises. But he probably didn't know it was in a blue box or anything like that, just that Flaxford had it and he couldn't let it fall into the wrong hands. At any rate, he sent over a pair of oafs to toss my place. If he did that, then he didn't get the box himself. And that means no one did."

"What about the killer?"

"Huh?"

"Flaxford had a visitor at his apartment that night. Someone he knew. Probably someone else he was blackmailing. Who knows how many people he had his hooks into? And he could have kept all the evidence in that box of his."

"Keep talking."

She shrugged. "So he met with his victim and the victim demanded to see the evidence and Flaxford showed it to him, and then the victim killed Flaxford, smashed his head in, and scooped up the box and ran like a thief."

"Like a murderer, too."

"Exactly. Seconds later you went in—it's a miracle you and the killer didn't bump into each other in the hallway, actually—and meanwhile someone heard the struggle and called the police, and while you were riffling desk drawers they came through the door and there you were."

"There I was," I agreed.

"This Debus would still think the box was either at Flaxford's apartment or at your place. Because he wouldn't know about X."

"About who?"

"X. The killer." I looked at her. "Well, that's how they always say it on television."

"I hate seeing my whole life reduced to an algebraic equation."

"Well, call him whatever you want. Just because Debus thinks you have the box doesn't mean a third person couldn't have it, so if you don't find it in the apartment it may be because it isn't there in the first place."

I felt slightly angry, the way people must have felt a few centuries back when Galileo started making waves. I said, "The box is in Flaxford's apartment." And the earth is flat, you bitch, and heavy objects fall faster than light ones, and quit raining on my parade, damn you.

"It's possible, Bernie, but—"

"The killer may have panicked and ran out of the apartment

without the box. Maybe Flaxford never showed him the box in the first place."

"Maybe."

"Maybe the blue box has been in Flaxford's safe-deposit box all along. Safe in the bowels of some midtown bank."

"Maybe."

"Maybe Michael Debus killed Flaxford. He got the box and then Darla Sandoval and Wesley Brill ransacked my apartment."

"You don't think—"

"No, I don't. Maybe Brill killed Flaxford because he couldn't remember his lines. He gave the box to Carter Sandoval to keep his coin collection in. That's not what I think, either. I'll tell you what I think. I think the blue box is in Flaxford's place."

"Because you want it to be there."

"That's right, because I want it to be there. Because I'm a fucking intuitive genius who plays his hunches."

"Which is largely responsible for the fantastic success you've made of your life."

We were by this point managing the neat trick of screaming at each other without raising our voices. In a portion of my mind—the portion that wasn't screaming—I wondered just what we were really mad about. I knew that on my part there was at least a little sexual agitation involved. Darla Sandoval had started fires that had not yet been properly extinguished.

Ultimately the fighting died down as pointlessly as it had started. We looked at each other and it was over. "I'll make coffee," she offered. "Unless you'd rather have a drink."

"Not when I'm working."

"But you'll have keys, won't you? And you'll be with an authorized representative of the law."

"It's still burglary as far as I'm concerned."

"So just coffee for you. Fair enough. He's picking you up at her place? Are you going uptown dressed like that?"

"Don't you think I'll be warm enough? Sorry. I don't know if I'll change or not. Frankly I'm getting sick of putting this uniform on and taking it off. But with my luck somebody'll stop me en route uptown and expect me to shoot it out with a holdup man."

"Or investigate a burglary."

"Or that. And without the cap the uniform looks incomplete. I guess I'll change."

"After you take your uniform off," she said, "would you have to put your other clothes on right away?"

"Huh?"

She turned toward me, gave me a slow smile.

"Oh," I said, and began undoing buttons.

Chapter Fifteen

I BEAT the cops to Darla's place, but not by more than a few minutes. I had barely finished changing into my basic blue when the doorbell rang. I opened the door to admit Ray and Loren. Ray looked sour, Loren uncertain. Ray came in first, pointing over his shoulder with his thumb. "He's been driving me nuts, Bernie," he said. "You want to tell him why he can't come along with us?"

I looked at Loren, who in turn looked at my scotch-grain loafers, not because he disapproved of them but because they were where he wanted to point his eyes. "I just think I should go, too," he said. "Suppose something happens. Then what?"

"Nothing's gonna happen," Ray said. "Me and Bernie, we're gonna visit a place, then we're gonna leave the place, then we come back here and Bernie gives you your stuff back and you and me, we get the hell outta here and go home and count our money. You bring some magazines along?"

"I brought a book."

"So you sit on the couch there and read your book. It's a nice comfortable couch. I sat on it earlier myself. You usually pick up this kind of dough reading a book?"

Loren breathed in and out, in and out. "Suppose something happens. Suppose this Gemini here pulls something and you and I are on opposite ends of town, Ray. Then what?"

"Flaxford's apartment's on the East Side," I pointed out. "Just like this one."

No one responded to this. Loren began describing things that could go wrong, from traffic wrecks to sudden civil defense alerts. Ray replied that having three cops along, two legitimate and one not, was more awkward than having one real one and one ringer.

"I don't like this," Loren said. "I'm not nuts about it, if you want to know the truth."

"If you came along, you and Bernie'd only have one gun between the two of you. And one badge and so on. Just one hat, for Chrissakes."

"That's another thing. I'm going to be sitting here without my badge, without my gun. Jesus, I don't know, Ray."

"You'll be sittin' behind a locked door in an empty apartment, Loren. What in the hell do you need a gun for? You scared of cockroaches?"

"No roaches," I said. "This is a class building."

"There you go," Ray said. "No roaches."

"Who cares about roaches?"

"I thought maybe you did."

"I just don't know, Ray."

"Just sit down, you asshole. Give Bernie your stuff. Bernie, maybe a drink would help him unwind, you know?"

"Sure."

"You got any booze around?"

I went into the kitchen for the Scotch. I brought the bottle and a glass and some ice. "I better not," Loren said. "I'm on duty."

"Jesus Christ," Ray said.

I said, "Well, it's here if you want it, Loren." He nodded. I buckled on his gun belt and made sure the holster was snapped shut so that the gun wouldn't fall out and embarrass us all. I reached back, patted the cold steel on my hip, and thought what a horrible thing it was. "Damned thing weighs a ton," I said.

"What, the gun? You get used to it."

"You'd think it'd be hard to walk straight, all that weight."

"No time at all you get used to it. You get so you feel naked without it, you know."

I took the shiny black nightstick from Loren and gave it an experimental whack against my palm. The wood was smooth and well-polished. Ray showed me how to hook it to my belt and fix the stick so it wouldn't swing loose and wallop me in the shin. Then I pinned on my badge, set my cap on my head and straightened it. I went to the bedroom and looked at myself in the mirrored door, and this time I decided that I really did look like a cop.

The cap helped, certainly, and I think the badge and gun and stick and cuffs made a subtle difference too, changing my own attitude, making me feel more comfortable in my role. I took the nightstick from its grip, giving it a tentative twirl, then tucking it back where it belonged. I even considered practicing getting the gun out of the holster but rejected the idea, confident that I would only succeed in shooting off a toe. Miraculous enough that I'd pinned my badge to my uniform blouse, I thought, and not to my skin.

But by the time I returned to the living room I felt enough like a cop to tell someone to move on, or hold up traffic, or get a free meal at a lunch counter. And I guess Ray noticed the difference. He looked me over from cap to shoes and back again and gave a slow nod. "You'll pass," he said.

Even Loren had to agree. "They're natural actors," he said.

"Burglars?"

"Geminis."

"Jesus," Ray said. "Let's get the hell outta here."

IN THE black-and-white he said, "We're cleared to enter the apartment. It's sealed as evidence but what we do is break those seals and affix new ones when we leave. It'll all be recorded that way so nothing'll be screwed up."

"Is that standard?"

"Oh, sure. The seals are to prevent unauthorized entry. They can't really keep anybody out who wants in but you can't go through the door without you break the seal. This particular apartment, it's been opened up and resealed a couple times already. I saw the sheet on it."

"Oh? Who's been inside?"

"The usual. The photographer and the lab crew went through it before it was sealed up in the first place, but then the photographer went back for seconds later on. Maybe some of his pictures didn't turn out or maybe somebody from the D.A.'s office wanted him to get establishing shots of the other rooms. You never know what those monkeys'll want to show to a jury and label it Exhibit A. Then there was another visit from an Assistant D.A., probably to get the feel of the place firsthand, and there were a couple of bulls from Homicide, even though this is the precinct's case all the way and we're not letting those pricks from Homicide take it away from us, but of course they have to get a look all the same, maybe figuring the M.O.'ll fit a case they're already carryin' on the books. Then, and it musta been the same kind of thing, there was a visit from another D.A.'s office, not even Manhattan but some clowns from across the river—"

"When was that?"

"I dunno. What's the difference?"

"Which office was it? Brooklyn? Queens?"

"Brooklyn."

"Who's the Brooklyn D.A.?"

"Kings County D.A. is—shit, I forget the name."

"Is it Michael Debus?"

"That's it. Yeah, Debus. Why?"

"When were his men there?"

"Sometime between the murder and tonight. What's it matter?" He looked at me thoughtfully, almost sideswiping a parked car in the process. "They park right in the middle of the fuckin' street," he complained. "How do you connect up with this Debus character, Bernie?"

"I don't. I think Flaxford did."

"How?"

I thought for a moment. If I knew precisely when my own apartment had been visited, and precisely when Debus had had the Flaxford apartment searched, then . . . Then what? Then nothing. It might help my theory in my own mind if I could establish that Debus had sent men to East Sixty-seventh Street before he sent them to West End Avenue, but it wouldn't really prove anything, nor would it demolish my theory if the timing was the other way around.

When all was said and done, the only really important variable was the box. Either I could find it or I couldn't.

"It might eventually be important," I said, "to know just who Debus sent to the apartment and when they were there."

"Well, it's a matter of record."

"You could find out?"

"Not right this minute, but later on. Sure."

"It'll be there anyway," I said.

"Huh?"

"Nothing."

I RECOGNIZED the doorman. But he didn't recognize me, and I decided that I would definitely have to remember him at Christmas. He held the door for us as he'd held it for me twice before, and while Ray chatted with him he paused twice to challenge people on their way into the building. Evidently he'd been reprimanded for letting me in, but at least they hadn't taken his job away and I was happy for him.

I didn't even get a second glance from him. I was wearing a uniform and I was standing there next to Ray, so why should he pay any attention to me?

We rode up on the elevator with a man dressed as a priest. I suppose he probably *was* a priest, but he looked less like a priest than I looked like a cop, so why should I take anything for granted? It occurred to me that clerical garb would make a good cover for a burglary. It would certainly get you past most doormen in a hurry. Of course it wouldn't do you too much good in the suburbs where the object was to avoid getting noticed in the first place, but apartment houses were something else.

Now in the suburbs a mailman's uniform would be ideal. Of course, a lot of people know their route man, but if you could pass yourself off as the guy who delivers parcels or special delivery letters or something like that—

"Something on your mind, Bernie?"

"Just thinking about business," I said. We got off at the third floor and left the alleged priest to ascend alone. I stood aside while Ray broke the seals on Flaxford's door. Then, while he was fishing in his pocket for the keys, I extended a finger and poked the doorbell. He gave me a look as the bell sounded within the apartment.

"Just routine," I explained.

"Police seals on the door and you think there's somebody inside the place?"

"You never know."

"That's crazy."

"Everybody has a routine," I said. "That's mine."

"Jesus," he said. He found the keys, poked one at the lock. I could see it wasn't going to fit and it didn't. He tried the other and it slid in.

"Must seem funny to you," he said. "Using a key."

Just a little earlier I'd used Darla's key and now we were using Flaxford's. The only place I had to break into these days was the place where I was living.

"Last time I opened this door," he said, "there was a burglar on the other side of it."

"Last time I opened it there was a corpse in the bedroom."

"Let's hope tonight's a new experience for both of us."

He gave the key a half-turn clockwise and pushed the door open. He said something I didn't catch and went on inside, reaching to flick on the light switch. Then he turned and motioned me inside but I stayed where I was.

"Come on," he said. "Whattaya waitin' for?"

"The door wasn't locked."

"Of course it was. I unlocked it."

"Just the snaplock. All you had to do was turn it halfway around and it opened. A lock like that has a deadbolt, too, and if the deadbolt's engaged you have to turn it one and a half times around to open it."

"So?"

"So the last person out didn't bother locking it with the key. He just closed it on his way out."

"What's it matter? Maybe his partner's got the key and he's halfway to the elevator so he doesn't bother. Maybe he never thinks to lock it with the key. A lot of people always leave their doors like that. They never take the trouble to use the what-chamacallit, the deadbolt."

"I know. They make my life a lot easier."

"So here we got somebody who it's not his apartment in the first place and he's gonna be slapping an evidence seal on it anyway, and what does he care about deadbolts? It don't mean a thing, Bernie."

"Right," I said. I poked at my memory, trying to catch something small and quick that kept darting around corners. "*I* put the deadbolt on," I said.

"How's that?"

"Once I was inside. I closed the door and I turned this gizmo here, this knob. That's how you engage the deadbolt from inside the apartment."

"So?"

"And when you and Loren got here with the key from the doorman, you had to turn it around a full turn to undo the bolt and then another half turn to draw back the spring lock."

"If you say so," Ray said. He was a little impatient now. "If that's what you say I'll take your word for it, Bernie, because I frankly don't make a point of noticing how many times I turn a key in a lock, especially when I don't know what the fuck's on the other side of the door, which I didn't at the time. None of this makes the slightest fucking difference and I don't know what the hell you're rattling on about. I thought you wanted to get into this place, but if all you want is to stand outside talking about bolts like a nut—"

"You're absolutely right," I said. I came all the way inside and closed the door behind me. And turned the bolt.

THE apartment didn't look different from when I'd seen it last. If the wrecking crew at my apartment had been Michael Debus's responsibility, he'd clearly assigned a gentler crowd altogether to the task of searching J. Francis Flaxford's digs. Of course the search of my place had been unauthorized and unrecorded while the visit here had been made with official permission and was duly noted in some official log. So Flaxford's books remained on Flaxford's shelves and Flaxford's clothes remained in Flaxford's closets and drawers. No one had slashed open his furniture or taken up his rugs or cast pictures down from his walls.

All of this seemed wildly unfair. Flaxford, who had gone to whatever reward awaits fixers and blackmailers, would never wear these clothes or read these books or inhabit this apartment again, yet everything was shipshape for him. I, on the other hand, had a use for the contents of my apartment. And I had been sorely mistreated.

I tried to put this inequity out of my mind and concentrate instead on searching the place. I began in the bedroom, where chalkmarks on the oriental rug (I've no idea what kind) indicated the position of the body. He had been lying just to the left of the foot of his bed, his outspread feet reaching toward the doorway. There were dark brown stains on the carpet where his head had been outlined and similar stains on the unmade bed.

I said, "Blood?" Ray nodded. "You always think of blood as red," I said.

"Brown when it dries, though."

"Uh-huh. He must have flopped on the bed when he was hit. And slid down onto the floor."

"Figures."

"The paper said he was killed with an ashtray. Where is it?"

"I thought it was a lamp. You sure it was an ashtray?"

"The paper said."

"A lot they know. Whatever it was, somebody musta tagged it and took it the hell outta here. Murder weapon, you don't go and leave something like that behind. It gets tagged and run through the lab sixteen different ways and photographed a couple hundred times and then locked up somewhere." He cleared his throat. "Even if something like that was here, Bernie, there's no way I could let you do nothin' about it. No tamperin' with evidence."

"I just wondered what happened to it."

"Just so you understand."

I brushed past him and moved around the bed to where an oil painting of a ramshackle barn hung in a heavy gilded frame. I realized that if there was a wall safe in the place fifteen people had already gone through it since the murder, but I moved the picture anyway and the only thing behind it was a wall.

I said, "Funny. You'd think he'd have a safe. A man like him would have cash around the house frequently. Maybe he just didn't worry."

"What cash? He owned property and he was in the theater, Bernie. Where does cash come into it? The only thing is the theater receipts and nobody brings those home nowadays. They go straight into the bank's night depository. Plus the little theaters he messed around with, how much money'd be involved in the first place?"

I thought, *Why bother going into it?* But all the same I said, "He was mixed up with a lot of characters. I think he operated as some kind of bagman or fixer. I know he was tied into some political heavies, but whether he just freelanced for them I can't be sure. Plus he screwed around with blackmail and extortion."

"I thought you didn't know him?"

"I didn't."

"Then where do you get off knowing all this?"

"The Shadow knows," I said. "The Department must know something about it, too, as far as that goes. Didn't you hear anything about Flaxford's secret life?"

"Not a word. But I don't guess anybody looked to find out. Seein' we knew who killed him and we got an airtight case, why futz around with details? What's the percentage?"

"Airtight," I said hollowly.

"Bernie, if you want to tell me what we're looking for—"

"*We* are not looking for anything. *I* am looking for something."

"Yeah, but what?"

"I'll know it when I see it."

"Suppose I see it?"

I made my way past him again, stepping gingerly over the chalkmarks as if the body itself were still there, an ectoplasmic presence hovering just above the carpet. I walked down the hallway, stopping to check out the bathroom. It was large in proportion to the rest of the apartment, suggesting the building had been divided into smaller rental units somewhere along the line. There was a massive claw-footed tub, an antique survivor that contrasted with the modern sink and toilet. I ran water in the sink, gave the toilet a flush, turned to see Ray looking at me with his eyebrows raised.

"Just remembering," I said. "If Loren hadn't taken a wrong turn after he flushed the toilet we'd have all been on our way."

"It's a fact. Who knows when somebody'd have finally discovered the poor sonofabitch?"

"Not for days, maybe."

"You'da been clear, Bernie. Even if we make the connection, what the hell can we do? Walk in with our caps in our hands and say we had you but we let you go? Besides, by the time it all comes together we wouldn't know if you were there the same night he got it, because with all that time gone you can't fix the time of death all that close."

"But Loren walked right in on him."

I stood for a moment in the bathroom doorway, turned toward the bedroom, then turned again and went back to the living room. I could check Flaxford's closet for false backs and bottoms but that just didn't seem like his style.

The desk.

I went over and stood next to it, started tapping it here and there. Darla Sandoval had seen him take the blue box from this desk and put it back in the desk when he was done showing its contents to her. And the desk had still been locked after Flaxford lay dead in his bedroom. I'd been through it once but those old fossils were loaded with secret compartments, drawers lurking behind drawers, pigeonholes in back of pigeonholes. The desk was where I'd been told to look in the very beginning, and it was where I was looking when Ray and Loren walked in on me, and it was where I would look now.

I got out my ring of burglar tools. "Sit down," I told Ray. "This may take a while."

IT TOOK close to an hour. I removed each drawer in turn, checked behind them, turned them upside down and very nearly inside out. I rolled up the rolltop and probed within and I found more secret compartments than you could advertise on the back of a cereal box. Most of them were empty, but one held a collection of raunchy Victorian pornography which had evidently been secreted there by a raunchy Victorian. I passed the half-dozen booklets to Ray, who'd complained earlier that Flaxford's shelves contained nothing more salacious than Motley's *Rise of the Dutch Republic* in two leather-bound volumes.

"This is better," he reported. "But I wish to hell they could write it in plain English. By the time you figure out exactly what the guy's doing to the broad you could lose interest."

I went on performing exploratory surgery on the desk. Now and then I removed an interior panel knowing I'd never be able to put it back later, and I felt sorry about this, but not sorry enough to cry about it. Eventually I realized that, however more secret compartments the desk might contain, Flaxford wouldn't have used any of them for the blue box. It would have taken him too long to put it away and get it out again.

I stepped back and looked down at the desk and wanted to wash my hands of the whole damned thing. The thought of washing my hands made me think of running water, which led me back to the bathroom in short order. While I stood there doing my Niagara Falls impression I found myself studying the elaborately inlaid tile floor beneath my feet. Old-fashioned clay tiles about an inch square, most of them white, with a geometric pattern traced in light blue tiles. When I got to where I was actually toying with the idea of taking up the floor I knew I was skating dangerously close to the edge. I gave the toilet a flush, rinsed my hands, looked without success for a towel, dried my hands on my blue pants, took Loren's nightstick from its clasp, slapped it briskly against my palm, and got out of there.

And turned left instead of right, tracing Loren's route into the bedroom. I went over to the closet and went through it very quickly, knowing I'd find nothing but clothes, and that was all I did find.

I was on my way out of the room when I happened to see it out of the corner of my eye, just a little scrap of something that had wedged itself between the bedpost and the wall.

I got down on one knee and examined it. I took a very careful look and I did some thinking, and it all fit with some thoughts I'd already had. I got up and left it where it was and went back to the living room.

I was sliding the final drawer back into the desk when Ray said, "What in the hell does *gamahouche* mean?"

I made him spell it, then took the book away from him and

looked for myself. "I think it means to go down on a girl," I said.

"That's what I figured. Why the fuck can't they just *say* that?"

"Other times, other customs."

"Shit."

I left him squinting at antique filth and did some pacing, then dropped into the green wing chair where I'd planted myself before tackling the desk in the first place. I swung my feet onto the hassock, took a deep breath, and again tried to put myself into the mood of the apartment.

Your name is J. Francis Flaxford, I told myself, *and you're sitting here comfortably in your bathrobe, except it's such a nice one you call it a dressing gown. You're supposed to be at the theater but you're hanging around with a drink at your elbow and a book in your lap and a cigar in your mouth and . . .*

"That's weird," I said.

"What is?"

"They must have taken both ashtrays."

"Huh?"

"There used to be a heavy cut-glass ashtray on this table."

"They found it in the bedroom. The one he was killed with, I told you they'd take that along and lock it up."

"No, there was a second ashtray," I said. "It was on this table here. I suppose it was a mate to the murder weapon. Why would they take both ashtrays?"

"Who knows?"

"Just super-efficient."

"Bernie, we're runnin' outta time."

"I know."

"And you didn't find what you were lookin' for."

"I found something."

"In the desk?"

"In the bedroom."

"What?" I hesitated and he didn't press. "Not what you're lookin' for, anyway. What are you lookin' for? Maybe I seen it myself."

"It's not very likely."

"You never know."

"A blue box," I said. "A blue leather-covered box."

"How big?"

"Jesus," I said. "Either you saw it or you didn't, Ray. What's the difference how big it is?"

"You say a box, hell, it could be the size of a pack of cigarettes or the size of a steamer trunk."

"About so big," I said, moving my hands in the air. "About the size of a book." I remembered Darla's words. "The size of a hard-cover novel. Or maybe as large as a dictionary. Oh, for Christ's sake."

"What's wrong?"

"I'm an idiot," I said. "Aside from that, nothing's wrong."

It took perhaps three minutes to find it, another five minutes to establish that all the other leather-bound volumes were what they purported to be. Flaxford's blue leather-covered box was nothing but a dummy book, a neat wooden lockbox that had been passing itself off as Darwin's *Origin of Species*. When it was open it wouldn't have looked like a book at all, just like a rather elaborate box which one might keep on a dresser top as a repository for tie tacks and cuff links and that sort of thing. Closed and locked and tucked away on a lower shelf, it looked no different from all of the real books which surrounded it.

The goons who went through my apartment would have found

the box. When they shook each book in turn they would have found one that didn't flip open, and that would have been that. But Flaxford's apartment never got that kind of a search.

"Aren't you gonna open it, Bernie?"

I glanced pointedly at Ray. I was in the green wing chair again and he was hovering beside me, gazing down over my shoulder. "You go back to your book," I said, "and I'll concentrate on mine."

"I guess that's right," he said, returning to his own chair and book. I kept my eyes on him and saw him peek over his porn at me, then resume the charade of reading.

"Back in a minute," I said. "Nature calls."

I walked right on past the bathroom and into Flaxford's bedroom, blue box in hand. Whether they look like books or not, those little home strongboxes are about as hard to get into as a stoned nymphomaniac. This one had a combination lock concealed behind a leather flap. You lined up the three ten-digit dials and you were home free. You pried the thing open with a chisel.

I wasn't in quite that much of a hurry and I did want the box to look as though it hadn't been opened, so I did a little poking and probing for a few seconds until the lock yielded. I had a look at everything that was in the box, then transferred all of it to my own person. My uniform had enough room in the pockets so that none of them wound up sporting an unseemly bulge.

When the box was properly empty I took hold of the bed and tugged it an inch or two away from the wall. The small rectangle that had caught my eye earlier was where I had left it, and it was a good deal more visible now that I had moved the bed. I used Loren's nightstick to coax it out into the open, then took it ever so carefully between thumb and forefinger, holding it by its edges and placing it into the legendary blue box.

And closed the box, and locked it.

On my way back to the living room I encouraged history to repeat itself, giving the toilet a convincing flush. Ray looked up when I returned to where I'd left him. "Nervous stomach?"

"Guess so."

"Nervous myself," he said. "What say we get outta here?"

"Fine. I can open this back at my place."

"I'd think you'd be in a hurry."

"Not that much of a hurry," I said. "I'm more anxious to get out of here. And Loren was unhappy about missing out on all this, so let's give him a chance to see what's in the box. I already have a pretty good idea what we'll find."

"And you think it'll get you off the hook?"

"It'll get me off," I said, "and it'll get somebody else on."

WE GAVE the place a lightning once-over to make sure we'd left everything more or less as we'd found it. The internal damage I'd done to the beautiful old desk didn't show, and the bookshelves looked quite undisturbed. Outside, Kirschmann affixed a seal to the door, noted date and time and added his signature. Then he gave me a deliberate smile and used the key to turn the deadbolt.

And, as the lock turned, the last piece fitted into place for me.

Chapter Sixteen

By the time we got back to Darla Sandoval's little love nest, Loren Kramer was a nervous wreck. I let us in with my key and when we came through the door Loren was behind it. Since we hadn't thought he might have chosen that spot for himself, we inadvertently hit him with the door. When he groaned Ray yanked the door forward and stared unhappily at his partner. "I don't believe this," he said. "I thought I told you to stay on the couch."

"I didn't know it was you, Ray."

"Hiding behind doors. Jesus."

"I got nervous, that's all. You were gone a long time and I started worrying about it."

"Well, Bernie here had to look for a box that wasn't there. It was sort of fun to watch him. He took a desk apart and everything. Then the box he was looking for turned up on a bookshelf. That's it right there. It was pretendin' to be a book."

"*The Purloined Letter,*" Loren said.

"Huh?"

"Edgar Allan Poe," I said. "A short story. But that's not exactly right, Loren. Now if you were to hide a book on a bookshelf, that would be like the story. Except this was a box that was disguised as a book."

"It sounds like pretty much the same thing to me," Loren said. He sounded sulky about it.

While we puzzled over all of this, Ray went to the kitchen and made himself a drink. He came back, took a large swallow of it, and suggested that it was time to open the box.

"And time I had my gun back," Loren said. "And my stick and my badge and my cuffs and my cap, the whole works. Nothing against you, Bernie, but it bothers me seeing them on someone who's not really a cop."

"That's understandable, Loren."

"Plus I don't feel dressed without them. The gun, we even have to carry them off-duty, you know. When you think of all the holdups foiled by off-duty patrolmen you understand the reason behind the regulation."

What I mostly thought of was all the off-duty cops who tended to shoot one another in the course of serious discussions of the relative merits of the Knicks and the Nets, but I decided not to raise this point. I didn't think it would go over too well.

"The box," Ray said.

"Couldn't I get my stuff back and then he opens the box?"

"Jesus," Ray said.

I hefted the box in my hands. "Surprisingly enough," I said, "this box isn't all that important."

Ray stared at me. "It was worth ten thousand dollars to you,

Bernie. That sounds pretty important. And it's supposed to get you off a murder charge, though I'll be damned if I see how it's gonna do that. For the sake of argument I'll buy that you didn't kill Flaxford. But I don't see you comin' up with a dime's worth of proof in that direction, let alone ten grand's worth."

"It must look that way," I admitted.

"Unless the proof's in the box."

"The box was a personal matter," I said. "Call it a favor for a friend. The important thing was for me to get into the apartment, Ray. I didn't even realize it at the time, in fact I actually thought that the box was the important thing, but just being in the apartment told me what I wanted to know."

"I don't get it," Loren said. He looked as though he expected a trick, as though when I opened the blue box I'd be likely to extract a white rabbit. "What did you find in the apartment, Bernie?"

"For openers, the door wasn't locked completely. The deadbolt wasn't on."

"Oh, Jesus," Ray said. "I told you some cop just shut the door and didn't bother locking it. What's it matter?"

"It doesn't. What does matter is that the deadbolt was locked when I let myself into Flaxford's apartment the other night. If it had just been the spring lock I'd have opened it faster, but that's a good Rabson lock and I had to work the cylinder around for one and a half turns. It didn't take me too long because I happen to be outstanding in my chosen field—"

"Jesus, what we gotta listen to."

"—but I had to turn the bolt first, then go on to knock off the spring lock. Which I did."

"So?"

"So either the murderer happened to take a key with him on

his way out of the apartment and then happened to take the time to use the key to lock Flaxford's corpse inside, or else Flaxford engaged that deadbolt himself by turning the knob from the inside. And I somehow can't see the murderer having the key in the first place or bothering to use it if he did."

I had their attention now but they didn't know quite what to make of it. Slowly Ray said, "You're sayin' Flaxford locked hisself in, right?"

"That's what I'm saying."

"Jesus, Bernie, all you're puttin' is your own neck in the noose. If he locked hisself in and the door's locked when you get there, then the bastard was alive when you let yourself in."

"That's absolutely right."

"Then you killed him."

"Wrong." I slapped Loren's stick against the palm of my hand. "See, I have an advantage here," I went on. "I happen to know for a fact that I didn't kill Flaxford. So knowing he was alive when I got there means something different to me. It means I know who killed him."

"Who?"

"It's obvious, isn't it?" I pointed with the nightstick. "Loren killed him. Who else?"

I WATCHED Loren's right hand. Interestingly enough, it went to where his gun would have been if I hadn't been wearing it at the time. He dropped his hand to his side and saw me looking at him and blushed.

"You're out of your mind," he said.

"I don't think so."

"If that's not typical for Gemini I don't know what is. Just try on any kind of a wild lie and see how it goes over. Ray, I think we better take him in. This time put cuffs on him, will you? He already escaped from us once."

Ray was silent for a moment. Then to me he said, "Are you just snowballing this one, Bernie? Puttin' it together as you go along?"

"No, I think it's fairly solid, Ray."

"You want to run it by me once just for curiosity?"

"Ray, you're not going to listen to this maniac—"

"Shut up," Ray Kirschmann said. And to me he added, "Go ahead, Bernie, you got me interested. Go through it once for me."

"Sure," I said. "It's pretty simple, actually. J. Francis Flaxford was supposed to go to the opening of a play that night. It was all set. That's why I picked that particular time to hit his apartment. I had inside information and my source knew for a fact he'd be out.

"Well, he was all set to go. He was in his dressing gown, ready to get dressed, and then he had an accident. I don't know if it was a stroke or a fainting spell or a minor heart attack or an accidental fall or what, but the upshot of it is he wound up passed out on his bed wearing his robe. Somewhere along the line he probably knocked the lamp off the bedside table or bumped into something and maybe that was the noise that prompted some neighbor to call the cops. It doesn't matter. The significant thing is that he was unconscious in his bedroom with the door locked from inside when I entered the apartment."

"This is crazy," Loren said.

"Let him talk." Ray's voice was neutral. "So far you're just spinnin' your wheels, Bernie."

"All right. I got into the apartment and went right to work. I never left the living room and did nothing but go through the desk because that was where the box was supposed to be. My informant didn't know the box was disguised as a book. I was still playing around with the desk when you arrived. We had our conversation, made our financial arrangements, and we were all set to leave when Loren got a call of nature."

"So?"

"So according to his story, he went to the bathroom, used the toilet, then made a wrong turn on his way back and walked to the bedroom by mistake. There he discovered Flaxford's corpse. So he turned and rushed all the way back to the living room where we were waiting for him, finally sounded the alarm far and wide, turned a little green around the gills and flopped over in a faint."

"Well, we both saw him do that, Bernie. And then you sandbagged me and took off like a bat outta hell."

I shrugged off that last charge. "Loren saw Flaxford right off the bat," I said, "speaking of bats. He had to. That's a short hallway. If you walk toward the bathroom from the living room you can see those chalkmarks on the bedroom carpet before you reach the bathroom door. Of course there were no chalkmarks at the time. But there was a body there, sprawled out on the bed, and that was interesting enough so that Loren passed right by the john and checked out the bedroom."

"And?"

"He was in there for a few minutes. Then the body—Flaxford, that is—came to life. I don't know whether Loren originally thought he was dead or unconscious, but either way the man was suddenly alive and awake and staring at him, and Loren reacted automatically. He swung his trusty nightstick and cracked Flaxford over the head."

"Crazy," Loren said. His voice was trembling but that might have been rage and indignation as easily as guilt. "He's out of his mind. Why would I do anything like that?"

"For money."

"What money?"

"The money you were filling your pockets with when Flaxford blinked his baby blues at you. There was money all over his lap and all over the floor when you found him." To Ray I said, "Look, Flaxford was a fixer, a bagman, a guy with a lot of angles going for himself. He may have bank accounts and safe-deposit boxes and secret stashes but he also would have had cash on hand. Every operator like that does, whether his operations are legal or not. Look, I'm just a small-time burglar myself but I was able to put my hands on ten grand tonight." I saw no point in adding that only half of it had been mine.

"Now the one thing that never turned up in Flaxford's apartment was money. Not in his drawer or closets, not in any wall safe, not in that fantastic desk. With all the searches that place got, including the search I gave it tonight, the one thing that never turned up was cash."

"So you're saying that because there was no cash Loren here must have taken it?"

"It's crazy," Loren said.

"It's not crazy," I said. "Whatever knocked Flaxford unconscious, it got him suddenly. A fall, a stroke, whatever—all of a sudden he was unconscious. It's my guess he had a recent visitor bringing him a payoff that he was supposed to transfer from one person to another. The payoff was big enough to make him delay his trip to the theater. He got the cash, his visitor left, and he took it to his bedroom to count it before he passed out. Loren walked in and found this unconscious man in a room full of hundred-dollar bills."

"You're guessing."

"Am I? My apartment got ransacked, Ray. Every drawer turned upside down, every book shaken open, the most complete search you can imagine. There's nothing in the blue box that could inspire that kind of a search. But somebody knew Flaxford had a lot of money on him when he was killed, and the person who would have made that assumption was the person who gave him the money. I think it was probably Michael Debus or someone associated with him. Either the money was being channeled to Debus or Debus was spreading it through Flaxford to head off an investigation into his office. But that explains why Flaxford's visitor couldn't have killed him, in addition to the business with the locks. That person—say Debus for convenience—left Flaxford alive and left the money with him. And the sum was large enough so that Debus wasn't willing to write it off after Flaxford was killed. It was even large enough so that Loren thought it was worth killing for."

"Ray, he's crazy. This man is crazy."

"I don't know, Loren," Ray said.

"You've got to be kidding."

"I don't know. You always liked money."

"You sound like you're starting to believe this fairy story."

"You always took what was handed to you, Loren. As green as you were I was a little surprised. Usually it'll take a while before a guy learns to stick his hand out. Then he sees how it's part of the system and he gets hardnosed in various ways, and little by little he develops an appetite. But you, Loren, you were hungry right outta the box. You were hungry without ever gettin' hip. You're still mopin' around with your moon in fuckin' Capricorn or whatever it is and you're the hungriest sonofabitch I ever saw."

"Ray, you know I'd never kill anybody."

"I'm not sure what I know."

"Ray, with a nightstick? Come on."

I was glad he'd brought that up. I swung Loren's nightstick and slapped it ringingly against my palm. "Nice club," I said. "Smooth and shiny. A person would swear you never hit anybody with it, Loren."

"I never did."

"No, you never did. Or bumped it into anything or dropped it on the pavement or scraped it against a brick wall. Or even wore it until a couple of days ago." I pointed it at him in a shamelessly theatrical gesture. "It's new, isn't it, Loren? Brand new. Positively virginal. Because you had to replace your old one. It wasn't brand new and it had been knocked around a lot because you liked to play with it and you tended to drop it a lot. The surface was chipped and there were a few cracks in it. And you knew Flaxford's blood could have soaked into the cracks—blood or skin fragments or something—and you have to know what a crime lab can do with something like that and that all the scrubbing in the world isn't always enough to get rid of the evidence. You got rid of the whole nightstick."

Loren opened his mouth but didn't say anything. Ray took the stick out of my hand and examined it. "It does look pretty cherry," he said.

"Ray, for God's sake."

"Very fuckin' new, Loren. This ain't the club you been carryin' around. When'd you get this one?"

"Oh, maybe a week, two weeks ago."

"Before the Flaxford murder, huh?"

"Of course before the burglary. Ray—"

"What was the matter with the old one?"

"I don't know. I just liked the heft of this one better. Ray—"

"You throw the old one away, Loren?"

"I probably got it around somewheres."

"You figure you could come up with it if you had to?"

"I guess so. Oh, come to think of it, I think I maybe left it out in the backyard. Of course one of the neighbors' kids might have run off with it but there's still a chance it's there."

The two of them looked at each other. I might as well not have been in the room. They held each other's gaze for a long time before Loren averted his eyes and examined his shoes. They were black oxfords, incidentally, polished to a high sheen and far more suitable for a uniformed patrolman than scotch-grain loafers.

Ray said, "The toilet. He went to the bathroom and we heard him flush the toilet and then just a few seconds later he was back in the living room. How'd he have time to do everything you said?"

"He flushed the toilet on the way back, Ray. He walked right past the bathroom originally and he just stopped on the way back to flush the toilet."

"As a cover?"

"Right."

"Yeah, I guess that would fit. What about the ashtray? Flaxford got killed with an ashtray."

"From the living room."

"How do you figure that?"

"You remember when I asked about the ashtray? There was

one in the living room on the table next to where I was sitting. It wasn't there tonight and I thought at first that it was the mate to the murder weapon, one of a pair, and the lab crew took both of them for some reason. But there was only the one ashtray. It was in the living room when I entered the apartment and by the time the lab crew got there it was in the bedroom."

"How'd it get there? He took it?"

"Sure. He came back to the living room and did his fainting act. It seemed strange the way that happened. It was the damnedest delayed reaction ever, if you think about it. Of course if he never saw a corpse before—"

"He's seen a few."

"Well, maybe this was the first one he was ever responsible for. So he probably did feel a little weak in the knees, but he managed to get all the way back to where we were and then flop on the rug. It wasn't a real faint. A minute later I was out the door, and then when you got yourself together you ran right out after me, didn't you?"

"So?"

"He was still on the rug when you took off. As soon as you cleared the door your buddy here grabbed the glass ashtray off the table and went back to the bedroom with it. Then he parted Flaxford's hair with it. Maybe he'd only stunned him with the nightstick. Maybe Flaxford was already dead but Loren wanted to supply a convenient murder weapon. I think he was probably still alive, but a couple of swipes with a heavy hunk of glass would finish the job. Then he could recover consciousness and rush out and join you on the street. He'd have the rest of the money picked up by then and he'd be home free, leaving me with a murder rap hanging around my neck."

I don't know exactly when Ray Kirschmann knew I was telling the truth, but somewhere in the course of that speech the last of his doubts vanished. Because I heard him unsnap his own holster so that he'd be able to get to his gun if he needed it. The gesture was not lost on Loren, who looked as though he was about to take a step forward, then changed his mind and sat down on the couch.

Ray said, "How much money, Loren?" And when Loren didn't answer he asked me.

"He'll tell you sooner or later. My guess is it's better than twenty thou and probably double that. It would have to be quite a bit to account for the way Debus is pressing to recover it. Of course Loren wouldn't have known just what it added up to until he got home and counted it, but he could see right away that there was enough there to kill for."

There was a long silence. Then Loren said, "I thought he was already dead."

We looked at him.

"He was sprawled out like a corpse. I thought for sure this guy killed him. I don't know what I thought. I started picking up the money. It was automatic. I don't know what came over me. Then he opened his eyes and started to get up and—see, all along I thought he was dead, and then he opened his eyes."

"And then you went back with the ashtray just to make sure, huh?"

"Oh, God," Loren said.

"How much did it finally come to, partner? Twenty grand? Forty?"

"Fifty."

"Fifty thousand American dollars." Ray whistled softly. "No wonder you weren't crazy about our deal tonight. Why take chances for ten grand when you already had fifty salted away, especially when you'd have to split the ten in half and the fifty was yours free and clear."

"Half's yours, Ray. You think I would hold out?"

"Oh, you're real cute, Loren."

"I was just waiting until I could find a way to explain it to you. I wouldn't hold out on you."

"Of course not."

"Twenty-five thousand tax-free dollars is your end of it, Ray. Jesus, here we have the murderer standing right next to you. It's open and shut and all he is is a fucking burglar, Ray. See how sweet it is?"

"Oh, I get it. You think we should hang it all on Bernie here." Ray scratched his chin. "Thing is, what happens when he tells his story? They'd lean on you and do some checking and you'd crack wide open, Loren."

"He could get shot trying to escape. Ray, he escaped once, right? He's a dangerous man. Listen to me, Ray. Think about twenty-five thousand dollars. Or maybe you should get more than half. Is that it? Ray, listen to me—"

Ray hit him. He used his open hand and slapped Loren across the face. Loren put his hand to his cheek and sat there looking properly stunned while the slap went on echoing in the silent apartment.

"You have the right to remain silent," Ray said after a moment. "You have the right to—oh, fuck this noise. Bernie, if the question ever comes up recall that I read this cocksucker his rights."

"No question about it."

"Because I want this to be airtight. I never liked the little shit but you'd think he'd know the difference between clean and dirty, between taking money and killing for it. You know what I'd like? I'd like something hard, some piece of evidence that would nail his ass to the wall. Like his nightstick with Flaxford's blood on it, but it's a sure bet that already went down the incinerator."

"You'll find the money. With blood on some of it."

"Unless he stashed it." He glared at Loren. "But I suppose he'll tell me where it is."

"He doesn't have to."

"What do you mean?"

"I don't think he actually picked up fifty thousand dollars. I think he picked up forty-nine thousand nine hundred."

"You lost me, Bernie."

I held out the blue box. "Now I didn't open this box yet," I said, "because I don't know the combination. But I could probably pick the lock, and when I do I have a feeling I know what we'll find inside. I think we'll find a hundred-dollar bill and I think there'll be a bloodstain on the bill and I even think there'll be a fingerprint on the bloodstain. Now it could conceivably be Flaxford's fingerprint if he did some bleeding before Loren got to him. Maybe he cut himself on the lamp as he knocked it over. But I have a hunch it'll be Loren's fingerprint, and it certainly ought to be a good piece of evidence, don't you think?"

Ray gave me a long look. "That's what you *think* you'll find in the box."

"Call it a hunch."

"So why not open the box and see for ourselves?" And when I'd done so he said, "Beautiful, just beautiful. When'd you set this up, anyway? Oh, sure, the time you went to the toilet. You faked flushing it same as Loren did. That's cute. And the bill was there all the time? The lab boys missed it? Amazing."

"It must have been in the blue box all along."

"Uh-huh. I don't suppose I'll ever learn what was really in the blue box, and I don't really suppose I give a shit. I like what's in there now. That's a beautiful print, all right, and I'll bet it does turn up to be yours, Loren, and I'll also bet that blood turns out to be the right type." He sighed heavily. "Loren," he said, "I think you're in a lot of trouble."

Chapter Seventeen

"THAT'S fantastic," Ellie said. "Just incredible. You actually solved the murder."

"That's what I did, all right."

"It's amazing." She drew up her legs and tucked her feet underneath herself. She was wearing the outfit she'd had on the morning she knocked the plant over, the white painter's pants and the Western-style denim shirt, and she looked as fetching as ever. "I don't see how you figured it out, Bernie."

"Well, I told you how it went. The main thing was realizing that the deadbolt had been locked originally. At the time I assumed that Flaxford had locked it on his way out, but of course he was in the bedroom then. Once I made the connection, there were two possibilities. Either the murderer was someone with a key, or Flaxford had locked it himself from the inside. And if Flaxford had locked up, then he was alive when I was in the apartment, and if that was the case only one person could have killed him."

"Loren."

"Loren. And if Loren killed him it was for money, and money was the one thing that wasn't turning up. And there just had to be money in the case."

"And you figured all this out while you were opening the door."

"I had it pretty much figured out before then. I wanted it to look like it was coming to me while Ray was around so it would be easier for him to follow the reasoning."

"And then you had the luck to find the hundred-dollar bill on the floor."

I let that pass. It was luck, but I'd been prepared to make my own luck. There was a hundred-dollar bill in my wallet right now, one of the pair Darla and I had split, and there was a little blood on it for decoration, and it would have gone into the blue box if the genuine article hadn't turned up behind the bed. I'd needed something to take Ray's mind off what was originally in the box and a piece of bloody currency had looked to have the right sort of dramatic value, something Perry Mason might wave about in a courtroom. Maybe that was why I happened to notice the bill Loren had actually left behind. Well, this way I could keep my own bill, at least until I found something to spend it on.

Ellie got up and went to the kitchen for more coffee. I stretched out and put my feet up on the coffee table. I was bone-tired and tightly wired all at once. I wanted to lie down and sleep for six or seven days, but the way I felt I might have to stay awake about that long.

It was getting late now, almost one thirty. Once Ray and Loren had gotten out of Darla's apartment I called her at home as we'd arranged, ringing twice and hanging up. A few minutes later she rang me back and I reported that I'd found the box and had the tapes and pictures in hand. "You don't have to worry about negatives," I said. "They're Polaroid shots. One thing, whoever took them had a nice sense of composition."

"You looked at them."

"I had to know what they were and I didn't trust myself to identify them by touch."

"Oh, I'm not complaining," she said. "I just wondered if you found them interesting."

"As a matter of fact, I did."

"I thought you might. Have you listened to the tapes?"

"No. I'm not going to. I think there should be a certain amount of mystery in our relationship."

"Oh, are we going to have a relationship?"

"I rather thought we might. Does your fireplace work or is it just for decoration?"

"It works. I've never had a relationship in a fireplace."

"I had something else in mind for it. I'm going to burn the pictures and tapes before I leave. They're half mine anyway. I spent all my case money getting them back and I want them out of the way as soon as possible."

"They might make interesting souvenirs."

"No," I said. "It's too dangerous. It's like keeping a loaded gun around the house. The possible benefit is infinitesimal and the downside risk is enormous. I want to destroy them tonight. You can trust me to do it, incidentally. I'm not a potential blackmailer, just in case you were wondering."

"Oh, I trust you, Bernard."

"I still have my cop suit. I thought I might leave it here. It would save dragging it back downtown."

"That's a good idea."

"And I still have the handcuffs and the nightstick, strangely enough. The cop they belonged to had to leave in a hurry and he won't have any further use for them. I'll leave them here, too."

"Lovely. If it weren't so late already—"

"No, it's too late. And I have some other things to do. But I'll be in touch, Darla."

"Oh, good," she said. "That will be nice."

I looked up the number of the Cumberland and called Wesley Brill to tell him that the whole thing was wrapped up and tied with a ribbon. "You're completely out of it," I said. "The case is solved, I'm in the clear, and neither you nor Mrs. S. ever got mentioned. In case you were worried."

"I was," he admitted. "How'd you pull it off?"

"I got lucky. Look, have you got a minute? Because I've got a couple of questions."

I asked my questions and he answered them. We chatted for a minute or two, agreed we ought to meet for a drink one of these days, albeit at someplace other than Pandora's, and that was that. I found Rodney Hart's number in the book, dialed it, heard it ring upwards of fifteen times, then got a cooperative girl at the answering service. She told me where to reach Rod—he was still in St. Louis—but when I got through to his hotel there he hadn't come in yet. I suppose the play was still on the boards.

I changed back into my own clothes and stowed my cop gear in Darla's closet. She had some interesting gear of her own there, some of which I'd seen in the Polaroid shots, but I didn't really have time to inspect it. In the living room I flipped through the photographs and piled all but one of them in the wood-burning fireplace, which I now transformed into a film-burning fireplace.

I added the cassettes, which smoldered and stank a bit, stirred the ashes when ashes there were, put on the air conditioner and left.

I took a cab downtown to Bethune Street and had a lot of fun telling the driver how to find it. I looked up at the building. There were no lights on in the fourth-floor apartment. I stood in the vestibule and checked the buzzer at 4-F. No name beside the button. I poked the button and nothing happened, so I opened the downstairs door in my usual fashion and went up three flights.

The locks were easy to pick. I let myself in and didn't have to spend too much time in there. After ten minutes or so I left, picked the locks shut behind me, and climbed another flight to Rod's apartment where Ellie was waiting.

AND we were both there now, sipping cups of coffee laced with Scotch and working everything out. "You're completely in the clear," she said. "Is that right? The cops don't even want to talk to you?"

"They'll probably want to talk to me sooner or later," I said. "A lot depends on what Ray ultimately decides to do. He wants Loren out of that uniform for good and he wants him to do some time in prison, but at the same time he'd probably like to avoid a full-scale investigation and court battle. I figure they'll probably work out some kind of compromise. Loren'll plead guilty to some kind of manslaughter charge. If he's inside for more than a year I'll be surprised."

"After he killed a man?"

"Well, it would be hard to prove all that in court, and it would be impossible to do without dragging in errant burglars and bribe-taking cops and corrupt district attorneys and other politicians, so you might say the system has a vested interest in putting a lid on this one. And Loren has fifty thousand silent arguments in his favor."

"Fifty thousand—oh, the money. What happens to the money now?"

"That's a good question. It belongs to Michael Debus, I think, but how is he going to come around and claim it? I can't see anybody letting Loren keep it, and I don't think Ray'll be able to grab it all for himself. I wish there was a way I could cut myself in for a piece of it. Not out of greed but just so that I could wind up close to even. This whole business is costing me a fortune, you know. I got a thousand dollars in front and gave it to Ray. Then Debus's men did a few thousand dollars' damage to my apartment and its contents, and finally my five grand case money went to Ray so that I could clear myself. It all adds up to a hell of a depressing balance sheet."

"Can you get part of the fifty thousand?"

"Not a chance. Cops don't give money to crooks. I'm the one person in the world who won't get a sniff of the fifty thou. I'll have to go steal some money in a hurry, though. I'm as broke as I've ever been."

"Oh, Bernie. Look what happened the last time you tried to steal something."

"That was stealing-to-order. From now on I'm strictly freelance."

"Oh, you're incorrigible."

"That's the term, all right. Rehabilitation is wasted on me."

She put down her coffee cup, snuggled up close, nestled her little head on my shoulder. I breathed in her perfume. "What's really amazing," she said, "is that the box was empty all along."

"Except for the hundred-dollar bill inside it."

"But before you put the bill in the box was empty."

"Uh-huh."

"I wonder what happened to the pictures."

"Maybe there never were any pictures," I suggested. "Maybe he threatened Mrs. Sandoval but never actually showed her any pictures. Because in order to take photographs there would have had to be a third person there, wouldn't there? And no extra person ever did turn up in this case."

"That's true. But I thought you said he showed the pictures to her."

"That's the impression I had, but maybe he just showed her the box and talked so smoothly that she was left with the impression he'd proved there were pictures in the box? That's possible, isn't it?"

"I guess so."

"So there probably were never any pictures or tapes in the first place. And if there were, it's academic because they're gone now."

"Gone where?"

"Up in smoke—that would be my guess."

"That's amazing."

"It certainly is."

"And everything's all cleared up? That's the most amazing thing of all. The police don't want to lock you up anymore?"

"Oh, there are a few charges they could bring," I said. "But I talked to Ray about that and he's going to get them quashed without any noise. They could charge me with resisting arrest and unlawful entry, but they're not really interested in that and they'd probably have trouble making the charges stick. Besides, however they decide to wrap all this up, the last thing they want is my testimony getting in the way."

"That makes sense."

"Uh-huh." I draped an arm around her, curled my fingers around her shoulder. "It all wound up nice and neat," I said. "I didn't even have to bring you into it. You're completely in the clear."

THE silence was devastating. Her whole body went rigid under my hand. I kept that hand on her shoulder and reached into my back pocket for the book I'd found in Apartment 4-F. I had the page marked and flipped right to it.

I read, " 'I was divorced four years ago. Then I was working, not a very involving job, and then I quit, and now I'm on unemployment. I paint a little and I make jewelry and there's a thing I've been doing lately with stained glass. Not what everybody else does but a form I sort of invented myself, these three-dimensional free-form sculptures I've been making. The thing is, I don't know about any of these things, whether I'm good enough or not. I mean, maybe they're just hobbies. And if that's all they are, well, the hell with them. Because I don't want hobbies. I want something to do and I don't have it yet. Or at least I don't think I do.' "

"Shit," she said. "Where'd you get the script?"

"In your apartment."

"Double shit."

"Just one flight down. Fourth-floor front. Very conveniently located. I dropped in on my way up here. I thought your cats might be hungry but old Esther and Haman were nowhere to be found."

"Esther and Mordecai."

"Since you don't have any cats it seems silly to argue about their names." I tapped the little paper-bound book. *"Two If By Sea,"* I said. "The very play our mutual friend's traveling around the country with. And the speech I read comes trippingly from the lips of a character named Ruth Hightower."

"Who told you?"

"Wesley Brill told me which play Ruth Hightower's a character in. But I thought to ask him the question in the first place. When I introduced you to him as Ruth Hightower he thought that was amusing. I suppose he thought it might be coincidental, but you were quick to switch the conversation around and give your real name. And the night before when we hit Peter Alan Martin's office I was mumbling some doggerel about one if by land and two if by sea and Ruth Hightower on the opposite shore will be, some Paul Revere crap, and you got very edgy. You must have thought I had everything figured out and I was just babbling. Then this morning you decided to tell me your real name."

"Well, it doesn't mean anything, does it?" Her eyes met mine. "I just got into a role and it took me a little time to get back to being me."

"It's more complicated than that."

"Oh, it's not so complicated."

"Oh, I think it is. You got into a role, all right. And it was easy for you to get into a role because you're an actress. That should have been obvious to me earlier than it was. Look how neatly you ran down Brill yesterday. You knew just who to call—first Channel nine, then the Academy in Hollywood, then SAG. I didn't even know what SAG was, I thought it was something women tend to do after a certain age, and there you were on the phone with them, dropping little bits of shoptalk left and right.

"The thing is, the whole business was lousy with actors and theater buffs from the beginning. Flaxford dabbled as a producer and real estate operator while he made his money in less respectable areas. Rod's an actor who talked about the great deal he had on an apartment because the landlord has a soft spot for actors. Darla Sandoval's hobby is theater; that's how Flaxford got his hooks into her in the first place, and that's how she found Brill and used him to hire me. And you're an actress, and that's how you knew Rod."

"That's right."

"But it's only the beginning. It's also how you happened to know Flaxford, and he was the one who introduced you to Darla. You didn't meet her downtown or you would have known her last name. But you didn't. It wasn't until you heard her first name this afternoon at Brill's hotel room that you realized how it all tied together. Once you knew that the Mrs. Sandoval we were talking about was a lady named Darla, then you decided you had a previous engagement and couldn't tag along to her apartment. Because she would recognize you and you wouldn't just be the nice young thing who dropped by to water the plants."

"What do you mean?"

"You know what I mean, honey." I stroked her hair, smiled down at her. "The blue box wasn't empty."

"Oh."

I reached into my pocket, took out the one photograph I'd kept. I looked at it for a moment, then showed it to Ellie. She took a quick look at it, shuddered and turned away.

"That's Darla," I said. "The one on the left. The other one is you."

"God."

"I burned the rest of the pictures. And the tapes. You don't have to hold out on me, Ellie. I know you were involved with Flaxford. I don't know whether you met him through the theater or because he was your landlord. He owned this building, didn't he? He was the legendary landlord with the soft spot for actors?"

"Yes. He found me this apartment. I didn't even realize at the time that it was his building."

"And he had you on the hook one way or another. I don't know what he had on you and I don't care, but it was enough so that you cooperated with Darla. Then the other night you were over at his place. The night he was killed."

"That's not true."

"Of course it is. Look, Ellie, Ray Kirschmann bought my explanation about how Flaxford locked himself in his apartment. But that doesn't mean *I* bought it. I was the one selling it. You were in the apartment with him. You had a key to the place, and not because he wanted you to water his plants. You were sleeping with J. Francis often enough to have a key of your own.

"And you were in bed with him that night. That's why you were confused when the papers described him as wearing a dressing gown. You said you thought you'd heard he was discovered nude. Well, that wasn't what you thought you heard. It was how he was when you left him." I took a sip of my coffee. "There was a time when I thought you might have been in the apartment while I was searching the desk. It seemed possible. You could have heard me at the door and ducked into a closet or something. Then you'd have stayed put until I got out of there and both cops went tearing after me, and then you could have gotten yourself. That possibility occurred to me because I couldn't figure out how else you knew about me and knew I was at Rod's place. But that didn't make sense either, and I was sure you'd left Flaxford with his clothes off. But then how did you happen to turn up here? It was enough of a coincidence that you and Rod lived in the same building and I picked his apartment to hide out in. But how did you know I was here and how did you recognize me? You must have called Rod and asked to borrow his apartment and picked up his keys from some other neighbor. But how did you know to do that?"

"Hell."

"I kept you out of it, Ellie. The cops don't know you exist and they'll never have reason to find out. But I'd like to know how it all fits together."

"You know most of it."

"I'd like to know the rest."

"Why?" She drew farther from me, turned her head to the side. "What difference does it make? I'll go back to my life and you'll go back to yours. I can leave now. There's a whole pot of coffee and most of a bottle of Scotch left so you'll be all right."

"I want to know the story first, Ellie. Before anybody goes anywhere."

She turned to look at me, a challenge in the blue-green eyes. Then she said, "Well, you figured out most of it. I don't know where to start, really. I was at his apartment that evening. You know that much. He had an opening to attend and he wanted me to go with him."

"The Sandovals were going to be there."

"That wouldn't have mattered. I'd seen her around, actually, and we'd talked once or twice before he put us together for the photography session. I just never heard her last name. There must be hundreds of people I know on a first-name basis only."

"Go on."

"I was up there and we went to bed. He was an awful man, Bernie. He was extremely cruel and manipulative. I didn't want to go to bed with him. I hadn't wanted to go to bed with Darla, as far as that goes. He was . . . I would have killed him if I were capable of killing anybody. I tried to do the next best thing. I tried to let him die."

"What do you mean?"

"We were . . . we were in bed, and I guess he had a heart attack or something. He gasped and collapsed on the bed. I thought he was dead, and it was horrible, but at the same time I felt a great rush of relief."

"But he was alive. Did you know that?"

She nodded. "I checked his pulse and his heart was beating, and then I saw that he was breathing, and I knew that I ought to call the fire department or an ambulance or something. Then I realized that I wanted him to be dead. I even felt cheated because he was breathing and his heart was beating. I thought of killing him, smothering him with a pillow while he lay there unconscious, but I couldn't do that."

"So you left him there."

"Yes. I just . . . left him there. I got dressed in a hurry. There were a few things of mine in his closet. I packed them in a shopping bag, put my clothes on and left. I figured maybe he would live and maybe he would die and he would just have to take his chances. I wouldn't call an ambulance. I'd leave it up to fate."

"Where did you go?"

"Home. My apartment downstairs."

"What time was that?"

"I don't know exactly. Probably around seven or seven thirty."

"That early?"

"It must have been. We hadn't started to get dressed and we had to be at the theater in time for an eight thirty curtain."

I thought about it. "All right," I said. "He was collapsed on the bed naked around seven or seven thirty. Somewhere along the line he came back to consciousness. He got up, picked up a robe and put it on. He looked around for you and you were gone. Where was the money?"

"What money?"

"The fifty thousand dollars Loren found."

"I don't know anything about it. There was no money in sight when I was with him. I don't know who brought him the money or where he got it."

"But you locked the door when you went out."

She hesitated, then nodded. "I didn't want anyone just walking in and saving him. I couldn't actually kill him but I could make it easy for him to die. Was that horrible of me, Bernie? I guess it was."

I left the question unanswered. "He probably already had the money," I said. "Sure. He realized you were gone and he looked in the closet and your things were gone, too, and he wanted to make sure you didn't decide to take along the fifty thousand bucks that Debus had passed on to him, or that he had picked up on Debus's behalf. Whatever. So he went to wherever he'd put the money and it was there, and then he got a little woozy and he went back to the bedroom and sat there with the money in his hand, and he felt rotten and he tried to get up and he knocked a lamp over or something, made a noise, maybe cried out in desperation, and then he collapsed on the bed again. That could have happened any time before my arrival a little after nine. Then he was unconscious while I riffled his desk. He'd have lapsed into regular sleep by the time Loren went in and started picking up what must have looked like all the money in the world. Then the commotion woke him and Loren went nuts and smacked him with his nightstick, and Flaxford closed his eyes for the third and final time that night, and after Ray and I had done our little pas de deux Loren went back and beat him to death with the ashtray."

"God."

"But how did you come into it again? How did you know I was in this apartment?"

"I saw you come in."

"How? You couldn't have followed my cab, and how would you know to follow it anyway? Besides you were down here all along. All right, you could have seen me from your window, you've got an apartment that fronts on the street. But how would you recognize me?"

"I saw you uptown, Bernie."

"What?"

"I went back uptown. I sat in my apartment for a while and then I started to worry about him. If he was dead, well, then he was dead and that was that. But if not I really had to do something for him. I took a cab back up there and tried to decide what to do. I didn't want to call him up and I didn't want to send an ambulance before I knew whether he was all right or not, and I just didn't know what to do. I sent the cab away and I was walking back and forth on the sidewalk in front of his building, trying to get up my courage to go inside. I had my key, of course, and the doorman would have let me in because he knew me. But I was afraid Fran would be furious with me if he was all right and knew I'd left him, and if he was dead I didn't want to walk in on him, and—God, I just didn't know what to do."

"And then you saw me go into the building? But you wouldn't have recognized me."

"It was later than that. I saw you come *out* of the building. You were moving at the speed of light and you almost ran right into me. You sort of dodged me and went tearing off down the street, and a few minutes later a policeman came tearing out after you, and then the doorman told me you were a burglar who'd been in Mr. Flaxford's apartment."

"And then what?"

"Then the other policeman came downstairs a few minutes later and they talked about how Fran was dead and you had killed him. I didn't know what had happened. I came back here and stayed in my apartment, and I was convinced the police would find out that I had been responsible, although I don't think I really was responsible, but I was getting increasingly paranoid. I kept going to the window and looking out for cops, and then I saw you walk right into the building and I thought I was going to die. I didn't know who you were or how you knew about me and I was sure you were coming after me to kill me."

"Why would I be after you?"

"How did I know? But why else would you be coming into the building? I locked all my locks and I stood at the door shaking like a leaf and listening to you come up the stairs. When you reached the fourth floor I nearly died, and when you went on up to the fifth floor I thought you'd made a mistake and you'd be back down in a minute. When you didn't come back down I couldn't figure out what had happened. Finally I went upstairs and listened at the two doors up here, and when I heard sounds in this apartment I knew you must be in here because Rod was out of town and the apartment was empty. I couldn't figure out what you were doing here but I went back to my own apartment and knocked myself out with a Seconal, and in the morning I bought the papers and found out what had happened and who you were."

"And then you called Rod and arranged to pick up his keys."

"I also found out that he knew you. I said I'd run across a fellow named Bernie Rhodenbarr and hadn't he mentioned that name to me once? And he said he might have, though he didn't recall, but that the two of you had played poker together a few times. So I figured that was why you'd picked this apartment." She took a deep breath. "Then I decided to come up here. I didn't know whether you had killed Fran or not. I figured he must have been dead before you got there, that he died because he didn't receive prompt medical attention and it was my fault. But then there was all that business about the ashtray and I wondered if maybe you had killed him after all. And then you and I met, and I guess it's obvious I was drawn to you and fascinated by you, and I got involved more deeply than I probably should have. And at the same time I had to play a part. I couldn't give you my real name or address at the beginning because if you really were the killer and I wanted to bail out, then I was better off if you didn't know who I was or where to get hold of me. And if the police caught you, you wouldn't be able to drag me into it."

"And then you told me your right name because you were afraid I'd catch you in the lie."

She shook her head. "That's not it. I just couldn't stand it when you called me Ruth. I hated it, and when we went to bed and you kept saying my name at critical moments it was absolutely horrible. And I figured you'd find out my real name anyway. By then I knew you hadn't killed anybody, I was really fairly sure of that from the beginning—"

"Your famous intuition. I knew you had to be involved to some degree, Ellie. Nobody trusts her intuition that much. You had to have something else to go on."

"Anyway, you'd find out my name sooner or later. Unless I just disappeared one day. But I wasn't sure I wanted to. And everything happened so quickly."

"Right."

"So now you know the truth. I did a fair job of blowing the whole thing when I almost let us into the wrong apartment, didn't I?"

"I'd have put it all together anyway."

"I suppose so." She looked off into the middle distance, and I guess I did, too. A silence descended and hung around for quite a while. Finally she broke it.

"Well," she said, "things worked out pretty well after all, didn't they?"

"In every way but financially, yes. You're clear, Darla's clear, and I am no longer wanted for homicide. I'd say things worked out beautifully."

"Except that you must hate me."

"Hate you?" I was genuinely surprised at the thought. "Why on earth should I hate you? You may have come up here originally out of curiosity and to make sure you weren't in danger, but after that you helped me a lot. Not as much as if you had told me all the truth at the beginning, but what kind of fool goes through life expecting honesty in interpersonal relationships?"

"Bernie—"

"No, seriously, I don't blame you. Why should you have opened up to somebody who might turn out be a murderer after all and who was certainly a convicted felon to begin with? And you did help me a great deal. I couldn't have straightened things out without your help and I probably wouldn't have tried. I'd have gotten in touch with a lawyer and tried to work some kind of a deal through Ray. So I'd have to be a complete moron to hate you."

"Oh."

"To tell the truth," I said, "I'm kind of fond of you. I think you're a little bit nuts, but who the hell isn't?"

"You know I was involved with Flaxford."

"So?"

"And you saw that picture."

"So?"

"It didn't bother you?"

"Not in the way you mean."

"How else could it have bothered you?"

"In the sense of hot and bothered," I said.

"Oh. I see."

"Yeah."

"Oh."

I tipped up her chin and kissed her, and that lasted for a time, and then she sighed and nestled in my arms and said it was funny how things turned out. "And now what happens?" she wanted to know.

"Things keep on keeping on, baby. You go on being an actress and I go on being a burglar. People don't change. Both of our careers may be slightly disreputable but I think we're stuck with them. And we'll see each other, and we'll see how it goes."

"I'd like that."

And I'd see Darla Sandoval, and I'd try to figure out a way to knock off her husband's coin collection without Darla guessing who did it. And I'd probably try to put my apartment back together again, and maybe the neighbors would overlook my alleged occupation in view of the fact that I confined my operations to the East Side where the *momsers* had it coming. And I'd probably go on playing poker and watching an occasional baseball game and pulling jobs when I had to. It wouldn't be perfect, but who leads a perfect life? We're all imperfect creatures leading imperfect lives in an imperfect world, and all we can do is the best we can.

I said some of this to Ellie, if not all of it, and we cuddled together, and at first it was just nice and comfy and gentle, and then it got to be a little more than that.

"Let's go to bed," she said.

I thought that was a great idea. But first I went and made sure the doors were locked.

About the
Author

LAWRENCE Block is one of crime fiction's most prolific and diverse writers. Over his long career, he has penned more than fifty novels and dozens of short stories, in addition to nonfiction books and screenplays. He's the creator of several different mystery series, ranging from entertaining and humorous escapades to gritty crime tales that illuminate the darker side of human nature.

Block was born on June 24, 1938, in Buffalo, New York. He attended Antioch College in Yellow Springs, Ohio, but left school before he graduated. During college, he knew he wanted to become a writer, and after leaving college he had no trouble starting along that path. He did not have aspirations of becoming a literary icon and was perfectly satisfied with the goal of writing to entertain. He chose crime fiction because he always enjoyed reading this type of book as a kid, and he also found it to be the genre in which ideas came to him most easily.

In the 1950s, Block went to New York City and found employment churning out pulp novels and short stories in the paperback industry under various pseudonyms. He also published stories in pulp crime magazines, including *Guilty*, *Trapped*, and *Manhunt*. After a few years of writing these cheapie paperbacks, which Block found to be excellent training, he wanted to write books under his own name. One of the earliest novels he published without a pseudonym was *The Thief Who Couldn't Sleep* (1966), featuring his first series character, Evan Tanner.

Once Block began writing under his own name, the books began appearing fast and furious. He wrote several other Evan Tanner novels during the 1960s and early 1970s. In 1976, Block wrote *The Sins of the Fathers*, starring an alcoholic ex-cop named Matthew Scudder, the first in what would become Block's most famous series. Between Scudder books, Block lightened things up by creating the suave, cerebral gentleman burglar Bernie Rhodenbarr. *Burglars Can't Be Choosers* (1977) was the first novel in the "Burglar Who" series, which highlighted Block's sense of humor and playfulness even amid murder and mayhem.

Throughout his career, Block has deftly switched back and forth among his various series. He says he writes about what he feels like, with no particular sense of obligation toward one character or another. He would choose to write next about whichever sleuth suited his mood at the time. Similarly, Block does not strictly plan out his story's plotline. He doesn't use outlines and prefers to let the tale take him where it will. He usually writes from home, but he has also taken advantage of various writers' retreats, where in a month he could often compose a complete book.

One commonality among Block's books is that all of his series characters are based in New York City. Block himself has lived in the city all of his adult life and knows the city inside and out, making it the natural place for him to set his books. He also finds that the Big Apple energizes his work. "I grew up in upstate New York, in Buffalo. But I remember when I was ten, my father and I took the train to New York for a long weekend. I probably fell in love with it then. As soon as I could, I moved here, and I've lived here most of my adult life." He says he would "be a fool" to set his work anywhere else.

In his limited spare time, Block maintains a blog and a newsletter on his website. He has been a dedicated racewalker and has completed walking marathons. His memoir *Step by Step* chronicles his passion for racewalking. He calls it "a year in the life of an aging and none-too-gifted racewalker." Block is also an avid traveler and has visited around 160 countries with his wife, Lynne. While Block always has several projects percolating, so far he's not saying which character he plans to write about next.